THE
TRINITY
KNOT

releasing the knot of silence

DONNALEE
OVERLY

Giro di Mondo

Giro di Mondo Publishing
Amelia Island, FL.

For permission, please write to info@girodimondo.com

Cover and interior design by Roseanna White Designs

First Edition, April, 2018
ISBN Trade Paperback -   ISBN-13: 978-0-9990514-3-6
E-Book- ISBN-13: 978-0-9990514-4-3

Library of Congress Control Number: 2017964461
 Printed in United States of America.

Published by
Giro di Mondo Publishing
Amelia Island, Florida
www.girodimondo.com

This book is dedicated to all women

Painting isn't an aesthetic operation;
it's a form of magic designed as a mediator between this strange hostile
world and us, a way of seizing the power by giving form to our terrors as
well as our desires.

~ PABLO PICASSO

Prologue

December 4, 2017

Gabby lifts her eyes from the crossword puzzle and listens more intently as the news reporter on the television reveals another sexual harassment story. This is a topic that has been given much interest in the past few months as allegations of harassment have been made by dozens of women involving high-profile politicians and businessmen. Some of these incidents occurred recently; however, others occurred more than twenty years ago. Why are women coming forward publicly with voices that have been hushed for so long?

Gabby bites on the end of her pen, the puzzle left abandoned in her lap. Her memory tugs at her, taking her back to a time when she was quiet and didn't use her voice.

PART 1

THE GAME

CHAPTER 1

Needing to divulge her ugly secret before it tears her apart, Gabby trusts the canvas before her, thinking it loyal. Quickly choosing her words, she fills her brush with the dark paint. Her brush screams her anger and rage as she aggressively smears the color. The canvas listens, intensely absorbing the paint, each fiber holding the nasty details. Next, the canvas accepts her sponge marks that cry her despair and defeat.

She steps back from the canvas, searching for answers. Her eyes open wider, and her stomach churns. Yes, the canvas has a reply but offers no friendly comfort. Instead, the composition taunts her. *You are so weak. You are a failure.*

The painting, dark and callous, has betrayed Gabby. It mocks her. Her eyes sting as she picks up her palette knife and slashes through the cloth. Running to the trash, she heaves the painting into the dirty plastic bin. Sobbing, she reaches for her knees. How has she allowed his aggressive act to go unpunished? She hangs her head.

October 17, 2016 (One day earlier)

Gabby is at the country club. Intent on learning to add topspin to her backhand, she scheduled a private tennis lesson with Brett Matthews, one of the instructors. He is the coach for her team of eight and is well-liked for his teaching skills and personality

Exhausted from the hour lesson, she gathers the last of the balls hidden behind the curtain of the indoor tennis court. She hears the rustle of someone approaching, and her nose detects his scent long before she is within his reach. The subtle, spicy aroma wafts to the inner circle of her mind. He stands behind her, his warm breath on her neck. Every cell in her body is tingling, proclaiming life, as her mind tries to tame the thoughts bouncing back and forth as if playing a game of ping-pong. He laughs lightly as his arms reach the wall, imprisoning her. There is no escape. Her head is spinning; however, it hardly compares to the rapid beating of her heart.

Quickly, his arms drop as his hand reaches into her bodice, cupping her breast. He coos in a low voice, "I like my women sweaty." Gabby doesn't understand why she cannot cry out to the men playing doubles on the adjacent court. Is she in shock? Where is her voice?

In an instant, his right hand lifts her tennis skirt, dips into her pants, and finds her core. "Turn around," he commands.

Gabby's hand holds a tennis ball, but as if paralyzed, her fingers release, dropping it. Likewise, the same numbness travels to her opposite arm, sending her racquet to the floor, making a loud echoing sound. As she turns around, meeting Brett's gaze, skillfully his hands slide her pants down to her knees. She wants to slap him and curse violently, but none of those things happen as she stands powerless staring into those eyes. The coolness of the rough green cement wall behind her is hard against her back as Brett positions his body closer.

She wants to believe that someone will come to her rescue, but all she hears are the voices and the repeated thump of the tennis ball on the next court. Her lips quiver nervously, and she thinks, *Oh, God, what now?* Secretly, she has had fantasies of a hot affair but never really dreamed she would follow through. But this is not an affair; this is rape. She does not want this, and she cannot stop it. She has no voice and no control.

Here she is, face to face with a young, muscular Adonis. Now hopeless to resist his advances, she is breathless and trembling. He presses his manhood against her and whispers in her ear about how happy he is going to make her. Seconds later, he is probing his member between her legs. She tries to push him away, but he is too strong and quick. He presses her even more tightly against the wall, and she feels the rough, cold surface tear away the skin on her lower back. His other hand goes under her thigh, lifting it higher so he is able to thrust deeper into her. Faster than she could ever fathom, she is taken. The rhythm of his movement ripples the curtain. He pulls down on her ponytail, lifting her face upward to meet his playful eyes.

He finishes with a grunt and a wide smile. "Fabulous, right?" he breathlessly says, and Gabby isn't sure if this is a rhetorical question. How is she to answer? He tells her to put herself together because he has another lesson coming onto the court.

With a quick movement, he jerks the small chain from around her neck, kisses it, and places it ever so casually into his pocket. Smiling, he says, "As a reminder." He begins to walk away, smirks, and looks over his shoulder at her. "When you want another hook-up, let me know."

Her feet are glued to the floor. He raped her. Why does his banter sound as if it was just casual sex between friends? Her head is spinning, and she is unable to recreate the scenario of events leading up to the rape. The walls are closing in around her, and her breathing is quick and shallow. Right now, there is only one thing that is obvious. There is no undoing what just happened; there is no turning back the hands of time.

Clearly, Brett has done this before. He was so quick and skilled. Gabby is a beautiful woman. She is tall and athletic with long, blond hair. Why Brett picked her as the benefactor of his sexual aggression, she will never know. Why didn't she stop this encounter by reacting with a scream for help? This will continue to haunt her as she will recount these brief few minutes over many hours, if not days, and possibly forever. She doesn't understand much now, but what she does know is that she needs a quick escape. The future is the only element of time that she can control.

Did she walk to her car? Her purse is in her lap. She turns around and finds her tennis bag in the back. How long has she been sitting here? She looks in the mirror. Who is that woman staring back? Her eyes are wild, and her hair is disheveled. The face staring back is unfamiliar, so she touches it and feels nothing. There is no crying, no anger, no remorse, and no denial. She is a victim, but she cannot see the situation for what it really is.

Time passes. The numbness lessens. *What do I do now? Do I report Brett to the club management? Will they believe me? Do I call the police? Will they believe me? Do I tell Richard? Will he believe me? Do I tell my father? No, he will be embarrassed that a King was so weak.*

She keeps questioning. *If it was rape, won't there be some sign of trauma? Wouldn't the men on the next court have heard something ... a scuffle or a cry for help?*

Why didn't she scream? Why couldn't she push him away? She allowed Brett to force himself on her. Who would believe her story? Nonstop, she flips through the pages in her mind of her meetings and previous lessons with Brett, placing the blame on herself for leading him to believe that she was sexually attracted to him. It must be her fault. What should she have done? No one would understand. She is a victim and is all alone.

Her hand goes to her neck in her old, familiar habit. She can think more clearly when she has that charm in her hand. She often takes the trinity knot between her fingers, swinging it back and forth on the chain, but this time when she reaches for it, her necklace is gone. Painfully, she remembers that Brett tore it from her neck. The gold chain is very thin, and it didn't take much effort to remove. He has no idea how much that necklace means to her. "I need to get it back," she says.

It was the day of her mother's funeral that Gabby retrieved that necklace from her jewelry box and tenderly clasped it around her neck. On that day, she needed to feel her mother's love like no other day before in her life, and she needed her mother to feel her love in return. Wearing the necklace helped Gabby to fulfill the deep void when she said a final goodbye to the most important person in her life.

The necklace had been a present.

"Happy birthday, Gabby," chirped Anna King while she opened the curtain and pulled up the shade. "I am so excited. My baby girl is sixteen," Gabby's mother proudly announced as she sat on the edge of the bed, wrapping her arms around her daughter and kissing her on the forehead. Anna was excited to hand her the small gold box. "Open it," she said.

Gabby sat up in bed, rubbed her eyes, and did as she was instructed. Inside was a small gold chain with a gold knot on the end. "It's a trinity knot," Anna explained as Gabby continued to look at the necklace and hold the knot between her fingers. "It is a very special symbol as it tells the story of our family. There are three ovals representing each of us, and the center circle that holds the ovals together is our love." Anna gave her daughter another hug. "You are now old enough to have experienced the value of family and what we have accomplished together. I want you to remember that every time you wear it," Anna said as she took the necklace from Gabby and placed it around Gabby's neck.

The necklace is made of gold, but it is more precious to her than if it were made with countless diamonds. Anna is gone, taken from this earth far too early, and Gabby has worn that necklace daily as a reminder of her mother for the past few years. Now, it is gone too.

The necklace isn't the only thing that she misses. She also misses her family of three. Why did her mother leave her? Her mother would know what she should do.

As she wipes the tear that forms in the corner of her eye, she also smiles, reminiscing about those mother-daughter chats. There was the time Gabby got her first menstrual period. Her mother reassured her, "You're not going to die. Every woman goes through this."

This was followed by the most devastating time—her first heartbreak at fifteen. She recalls her panic and hurt as she was sure when Tim dumped her, her world had ended. She still hears her mother's soothing voice, "It's okay to be sad. The sun will shine again and you will be so much wiser having walked through the rain."

The memories warm her heart as she cherishes them, but today they also make her feel more alone, especially now that her world has collapsed. Thinking of the necklace, her mother, and the carefree days on the ranch, Gabby cries.

Brett puts away the last of the tennis balls and walks to the locker room to shower. His lessons have finished for the day, but he doesn't have that feeling of exhilaration that usually accompanies him after a new sexual encounter. This time, it felt different. Something went wrong. Usually he flirted more, took things more slowly, but in the end, the women always seemed happy and most wanted more. The result was always the same, so why not just go for it?

He stands in the hot shower and enjoys the water flowing from his head to his feet. The warmth is delightful after his busy day. Even though his muscles start to relax, his mind is still occupied with the situation on the court with Gabby. *Why was it different?* Usually, his women would speak of the excitement of the unexpected and of the thrill. Some shared with him afterward that it was the best sex they'd had in years. He seldom heard a complaint, except from women who wanted a more leisurely affair instead of the fast sexual interludes that he preferred. However, when he looked into Gabby's eyes earlier, excitement was not what he found, but rather a wounding, similar to an animal aware it was going to slaughter. If he were truly honest with himself, digging deep into his psyche, he would admit that this was a turn-on. So much so, the idea of being the conqueror excited him.

This time with Gabby King, he couldn't have stopped. Maybe this time he stepped over a line. Slowly, he reaches to turn off the water, grabs his towel, and heads back to his locker. After having unemotional sex for so long with so many women, has he become a dark, hard-hearted creature instead of the attractive, please-screw-me guy that women crave? Has he unleashed a monster that should have stayed caged in the deep abyss of the back corners of his mind?

He remembers the small gold necklace he confiscated. He removes it from his pocket, caresses it, and smells it as the faint scent of Gabby's perfume still lingers. He runs the chain between his fingers, examining each link, cherishing that each enclosed circle was witness to his awesome act. Eventually, this chain will go into the black box that holds the mementos he has taken from other women; however, for now, he wants to keep the chain close as a reminder of Gabby and of the situation he so carefully orchestrated and successfully performed. He is considering an encore.

He has known about Gabby and the wealthy prominent King family since he was a young boy.

"Folks, get ready. The junior calf roping is next," the announcer

broadcasted to the crowd in the arena. "The roper must lasso the calf, dismount, flip the calf, and tie three of its legs together. The current world record is just over six seconds. How close can these young cowboys come to matching that time?"

On the arena floor, behind the gate, a man patted his son on the shoulder. "You ready?" he asked.

Fourteen-year-old Brett Matthews removed his hat and wiped his forehead with the sleeve of his plaid shirt. He had prepared well for this moment. "Ready as I'll ever be."

The father gave more advice to break the awkward silence as he adjusted the boy's hat. "Focus. You can do this."

Hearing the announcer call his name made Brett's ears tune in.

"This young teen is the one to watch. He's had a stellar season. If this performance equals his previous, the other competitors will go home with their tails between their legs."

Brett took another deep breath and let it out slowly as he mounted his quarter horse. His white knuckles held the reins. His piggin' line was clenched between his teeth.

Later, standing in the arena, his heart skipped joyfully upon seeing the wide smile on his father's face. He accepted his ribbon for saddle broncing and his trophy for calf roping with pride, honored to claim the hardware as evidence of his hard work and skill. His eyes glanced down into the face of the Rodeo Princess as she handed him his treasures, making him blush. Her beauty was obvious even at her young age, and he knew that she deserved the crown seated on her head.

"Hold your trophy lower. Trust me. You will want the Rodeo Princess *in your picture," Mr. Matthews commanded his teenage son. Brett had thought that silly at the time. Why would he want her in the snapshot?*

He didn't know her name or her age, and he didn't care. It was all about that trophy, but how could he avoid noticing those soft eyes and that smiling face? Later, anxious to see his name, he read articles, learning she was the daughter of Mr. King, who owned the neighboring ranch.

<hr />

In the next few days, just as Gabby had allowed Brett to touch her without fighting back, she allows the days to come and go. She isolates herself from everyone by locking herself in her condo. She avoids going to work by complaining of having the flu. Thankfully, Richard, her boyfriend, is out of town. Having sex would push her over the edge in her fragile state. Her mind drifts, making concentrating difficult. Her memory is so consumed by the episode with Brett that she can't do the mundane things of the day. When she reads a book, she just stares at the same page and has to reread. She tries watching television but quickly forgets the storyline.

Her thoughts drift to Richard. Her dad set them up together. Her membership to the country club is paid by her father, as he wants her to find a man worthy to wed into their family. Wayne King was right because shortly after joining, an up-and-coming lawyer, Richard Wright, started dating King's twenty-seven-year-old daughter. The happy couple skipped the formal engagement process and moved in together. However, over the past two years, the relationship has gone under some strain as Richard works many hours each week and travels unmercifully to meet with clients.

Advancing his career at the law firm takes all of Richard's energy and time. He is a work-oriented man, and playtime just doesn't have the same appeal. Even in the hours away from his desk and courtroom, he focuses on work as his mind is ruminating and rehearsing his opening and closing statements for his next case. On a personality scale, Richard would score with the introverts. In his downtime, he enjoys staying at home with a good book or watching a detective drama on TV, rather than going out to a social event.

However, some influential men, including King, have a different plan for Richard. After there was talk that the current aging state senator was giving hints that he's ready to retire, the oil and gas businessmen are in need of a replacement who will represent them and uphold their interests. These men have approached Richard in the past with their idea, and he led them to believe that he was a viable candidate. Launching into the political arena is only a job for an extrovert, though, so he may be forced to step outside his comfort zone or level with the men and tell them he is not the man for the job.

Shaking away thoughts of Richard, Gabby quickly busies herself. Her need for activity is intense, so she cleans. She washes the floors and scrubs the bathrooms. Their sparkle and shine give reassurance that she will get through this. She cleans every drawer and closet. When she opens them, she enjoys the perfect stacks of clothing, wishing her life to be as perfect. Being busy creates a diversion and keeps her mind from going back to the incident on the tennis court, which reminds her that her life is anything but perfect.

She seldom answers the phone now. She allows the calls to go to voicemail. On the rare occasion when she does answer, she is a master at faking a cheerful tone. She is an expert at getting others to engage in long conversations as she will just ask a question and wait. If a team member calls about tennis, Gabby says, "Tell me about your match," or asks, "How did that happen?" Most people, including Richard, ramble on and on when given the opportunity, thus relieving her of the pressure of making conversation.

Normally, she plays tennis every morning. She is a member of several leagues, playing doubles and singles. Now, she has not gone to the club for almost a week. Thank goodness for modern technology allowing her to continue hiding, secluding her from the outside world. It is so easy to send an e-mail or text the lie that she is ill or something came up last minute, preventing her from joining others on the court. Gabby texts the club, *So sorry, but I will be unable to attend the drill today. Got the flu.* Or, *Have an appointment.* She easily finds subs to fill in for her. If she stays alone, inside the walls of her house, she can delay everything, including her next move, as she has no clue what that move should be.

Sometimes in life, not making a decision is making a decision. By not reporting Brett, Gabby has allowed the element of time to weaken her case. She has no evidence of rape or a struggle other than the abrasion on her lower back. She thinks, *If I report the rape, it would be my word against his. Who will believe me? I have no witnesses. I have no injuries.*

Now adding the passage of time, her case is greatly injured. She is enveloped in both shame and guilt, both useful tools the abuser is privileged to have in his corner to keep his victim silent. She tells herself, *I need time, time to think, time to make a plan, time to heal.* But time is drifting along, leaving her in its wake.

Suddenly, her phone rings, interrupting her thoughts. On the other end is her tennis partner and best friend, Ella Bender. They have been friends since they attended college at the University of Texas. No one would accidentally think them to be sisters as they are exact opposites. While Gabby is tall and blond, Ella is short and her face is framed by short, wavy brunette hair. Gabby decides to pick up this time.

"Hey, Gabby, missed you at tennis this week ... you okay?" Ella inquires.

"Just under the weather," Gabby says, faking a cheerful tone as she clenches her jaw.

"You missed a great match. I'm near your condo. Can I come over?"

Gabby does not want to be around anyone. She is tempted to tell Ella about Brett as they share everything. But she also wants to push the rape back far in her mind, and sharing her secret may cause some problems. *What would I do if Ella insisted on calling the police or worse, tell Richard?* On numerous occasions, Ella has shared with Gabby that she thinks Richard walks on water and is jealous that Gabby has landed him instead of her. Ella has praised Richard for his looks and his intelligence. *Yes, it's best to keep silent.* Using her excuse about having the flu, Gabby sighs in relief that she is able to turn Ella away without much effort.

CHAPTER 2

While sitting at the register in the art gallery the next day, Gabby's boss and friend, Rita Adams, lovingly gazes at her, asking, "What's wrong, Gabby? You haven't been yourself now for days. I know you had the flu, but this seems to be more than that. You seem to have lost your smile. You know you can talk to me. Is that boyfriend of yours treating you okay?"

Rita is the sole owner of the local art gallery. Gabby works there part-time to subsidize her income as an artist. It has been close to two years since Gabby waltzed through the threshold of the store in hopes of selling her art. Previously, she had tried to make the art scene in New York City's SoHo district, but after struggling for a year with little advancement in her trade, Gabby was encouraged to come back to Texas by her father, who was lonely.

Her arrival at the gallery was perfect timing as Rita's front clerk had just given her two-week notice. The girl was marrying a marine. She would be off to travel the world and follow her man—all in the name of love. Rita had shared with Gabby how this reminded Rita of her own carefree days of youth and the quest to find love. Rita, also a hopeless romantic, was happy for the girl and prayed all would be just as wonderful as the girl dreamed.

Gabby is reminded of their first meeting as she looks at the appointment schedule.

"Let me see what you have there," Rita said, reaching out her hand. Gabby confidently handed over her portfolio. This should be easy, she thought, comparing this interview to the drilling squad she faced marketing her art in New York City. She let out a slow breath as she observed Rita's head nodding in approval.

"These are impressive. I like the free spirit of your work. It is moving and evokes contemplation," she added while closing the folder and handing it back. "King, right?"

Gabby nodded.

"Any relation to the oil and cattle baron, Wayne King?"

Gabby looked down at her lap before responding. She wanted to get a job based on her own merit, not on her family's notoriety. However, it was a small town.

"No need to be ashamed. I like your humility. Too many kids your age act entitled these days," Rita interjected. Gabby looked up once again.

From the smile that crossed Rita's face after Gabby disclosed that she was King's daughter, Gabby was sure Rita thought that employing her would be a great asset as she would bring in clients.

"With the economic recession, the store is under financial strain. I

can't pay you much, only minimum wage," Rita sadly informed her. Then, removing her glasses and pointing her finger at Gabby, she continued, "But this is what I am offering." She sat back in her chair. "I really like your work, and I need the help. I can give you wall space in exchange for your help to manage the store. You can paint here in the back. That's why I put those bells on the door." Now, it was Rita's turn to show humility. "I know it isn't much. How about I throw in your own personal show? You give me the dates, and I'll get it on the calendar. Think it over, and let me know," she said, standing up to shake Gabby's hand.

Later, Rita shared with Gabby that she needed the gallery to succeed as Rita was in her early fifties and supported herself. Her husband, a military man, died some twenty years ago, and she never remarried. Her sons have moved on with their lives, leaving Texas, venturing to jobs on the East Coast. Rita visits them several times a year, but she prefers the warm days of a Texas winter to shoveling snow in freezing temperatures. Rita naturally takes on the role of a mother to Gabby, and Gabby is the daughter Rita never raised. The job arrangement works well at meeting both of their needs.

For Brett, life goes on as usual. Daily, he is at the club, working the desk, flirting with the gals, giving tennis lessons, and holding clinics. Handsome, with his tall stature and thick, curly brown hair, he wasn't always a smart dresser, but he finds that women enjoy a clean, well-dressed man. Add some cologne, and women swoon over him. He enjoys it, loving all the attention he receives, soaking it up much as an outdoor tennis court holds the heat radiated from the sun.

He needs his job, but it doesn't provide him with the lifestyle that he dreams of or the ones he sees that his clients have. One could say that he is a bit jealous and that jealousy is one of his motivators for initiating and accepting sexual advances.

When he plays the game right, he escorts women to lunches, dinners, and movies. It is always on their dime. Frequently, he arrives at the club to find gift cards in his mail slot, always disguised in an envelope, but many times he wonders if the other employees can smell the envelopes drenched in expensive perfume. These love notes thank him for a wonderful time and usually hold requests for future outings. He prides himself in his climb up the social ladder. Life now is certainly better than what it has been in the past. One of the women that he services regularly at "lunch rendezvouses" surprised him to the point of speechlessness. He had thought he was doing well when the Tag watch showed up after arriving at a hotel for a private lesson with the wife of one of his best clients. However, the gift that aced his world was delivered on his birthday last year. He woke that day, not only starting a new decade but as the owner of a red Audi sports car parked in his driveway.

Explaining the car to friends and family took cleverness, more than any of his previous gifts had. Many wanted to know how he could afford such a fine car on his measly income. Some asked Brett if he had taken to dealing in illegal activity. That remark would cause him to grin—a grin as wide as the state because, even in the great state of Texas, polygamy isn't even prosecuted. He is just having fun, casual sex, but he would be lying if he said he didn't worry that a drunken, unhappy husband with revenge on his mind and a gun in his hand would make him dance his last dance.

After receiving such an expensive car, Brett did not like the feeling that he might be losing control, since his acceptance of the car mistakenly gave the buyer the false impression that she should be his first and only priority. Quickly, Brett had to rectify that misapprehension, as he is not owned by anyone. He is the boss, not to be ordered around by some bitch he rolls in the sack with every now and then. This makes him realize that even though he enjoys his climb up the social ladder with the attention and gifts he receives, he also needs control, and the thought of having power is very appealing.

His need for control in the past got so intense that instead of pursuing a career as a rodeo competitor, he traded his ropes for a tennis racquet. However, even greater than the need for control was his need to distance himself from the pain.

As a young teen, rather than face the truth, he had felt a need to escape the ranch. But how?

Working alongside his father in the stable, Brett said, "Dad, I'm quitting the rodeo."

Mr. Matthews leaned on his pitchfork and asked, "You're kidding, right?"

Brett looked down. "No, I'm not kidding," he said as he shoveled more of the fresh hay into the stall. "The rodeo scene is getting old. I need something new."

Mr. Matthews said, "Hell, if I had half the talent you have, boy, I would ride forever. You could win lots of money for those few seconds in the arena—more money than I earn working here." He scratched his chin and looked at his son. "I want the best for you, son. I want you to have a better life than me. The rodeo is your ticket. This idea of quitting is foolish."

Brett faced his father with a stern look. "The coach thinks I could be good enough to go to college on a scholarship playing tennis. I could go to college, Dad. That would be a better life, right?"

"Going to college would be wonderful, don't get me wrong, but do you have to give up the rodeo? Can't you do both?"

"The tennis team practices one hour before school and two hours after school. There isn't time for both. Last I knew they don't give scholarships for cattle tying and bronco bucking."

His father continued spreading the hay in the stall. "I would hate for you to give it up. You are so good. Son, you're the best. Your mamma would be so proud. Tennis? I didn't even know that you played."

"I'm pretty good and I like it," Brett said. "We can't afford college, so if I can get this scholarship, that will be great, right?" He looked to his dad for approval.

"You know I love you, and I want you to be happy. You're right, paying for college will be a hardship. Back in my day, most men didn't even think about college." Silence followed as they continued with their chores. Minutes passed with no words exchanged. Then Mr. Matthews said, not looking at his son, "You're old enough to start making your own choices."

Although his dad was disappointed that he would no longer compete in the rodeo, Brett was relieved that his dad was allowing him to make the change.

Brett's college argument was a good one, but his father was still confused as to this sudden change. His son had the skills that would take him far. He was so proud of everything he had accomplished. Why was he quitting? Even though in a short time, Brett's dad saw his son excel in his newly chosen sport, Mr. Matthews never really understood the switch.

CHAPTER 3

While executing his sexual fantasy with Gabby, a fantasy he
had envisioned a thousand times previously, he saw her
despair and hopelessness, reminding him of a portion of
himself that he wanted locked away. He is all too familiar with that
look: the baffled stare, the hanging head, and the lack of ability and
efficiency. He portrays the image on the outside of a confident man
and an ambitious tennis pro when, actually, on the inside he struggles
with insecurity and low self-esteem. It was during that instant of
Gabby's complete surrender that these inner nagging feelings were
replaced with feelings of victory, making him feel more alive than he
had ever felt before.

By taking her so aggressively, he thought he was pushing himself
further from the past, further from his pain and humiliation, when

in reality, he unlocked a cage deep in his being, and that wounded animal was unleashed. The look in Gabby's eyes for those brief seconds made him remember a time when he was the victim, bringing back the past he desperately tries to forget. However, within seconds, he then became the victorious conqueror. His entire body, mind, and soul were absorbed, and time stood still. He had revenge, and in that moment of climax, he felt complete.

Is he forgetting the lessons he learned from his college tennis coach? This isn't the first time this wounded animal has shown itself. He is not a stranger to self-destructive behaviors. After leaving the ranch and then losing his dad just three years later, Brett, desperate for a father figure, found some stability in his college tennis coach.

"Brett, come here, son," Coach Miller said, rubbing his chin. "You missed curfew. I understand a fight broke out and that there were drinking and women involved."

Brett looked down at his feet. "It won't happen again, sir."

"You told me that the last time and the time before that," Coach Miller said, shaking his head. "You have the potential to be a great tennis player, but this reckless behavior has got to stop. As we discussed before, behavior invokes consequences. I have no choice but to bench you this week. You are a valuable member of this team. I had hoped that being needed by the team might be enough to motivate you to respect yourself more. What is going on with you?"

Coach Miller stood closer and placed his arm around Brett. When he saw Brett step away quickly, he suspected his young tennis player might have some unresolved issues. Coach Miller adjusted his stance so he could face Brett again but maintained some distance. "If you need someone to talk to, you know I'm here for you."

Brett never revealed his past. However, over time the coach could see that Brett was reclaiming his life and beginning to trust others. And as he excelled in tennis, his self-confidence increased, and his past was driven further away. Now, after forcing himself on Gabby, is he returning to those dark days?

In the past, he viewed his approach to sex as playful and adventurous. But maybe this time he went too far. His initial goal of having fun, impromptu sex turned into something much darker. He is aware that a person who has a history of being abused is the one prone to abuse others. His eyes open wide, and he shakes his head in disbelief when realizing that he has become this person. This element makes this sexual encounter different from all of the others. In his subconscious attempt to stop his own pain, he has hurt another.

This feeling of concern and care for another individual is new to Brett, and this is the first time he has ever experienced feelings of remorse. Patting his chest pocket that holds its treasure, he needs the security of knowing that Gabby's necklace is still there. Reaching for the chain, he holds it up to the sun's rays, each golden link glimmering and shining. It reminds him of Gabby's warm personality. Not only is she beautiful and from a very influential family, but she is friendly and kind to all who cross her path. On the chain is a small gold knot. Brett has seen this symbol before in tattoos on friends and in books, but he does not know the meaning. He holds up the knot, searching for any engraving or another identifying mark, but there is none, and he wonders how this necklace came into Gabby's possession.

He thinks aloud, "Does it mean as much to her as it means to me?"

Again, he smells the chain, but to his disappointment, the lingering fragrance is no longer present. He frowns as he continues to roll the chain between his fingers. He remembers that this necklace has touched her skin. He tries to visualize Gabby wearing it and nothing else. The thought arouses him, and he smiles as he places the necklace ever so carefully back in his pocket. Someday, and hopefully soon, he will place this necklace around her neck as his arms encircle her naked body, giving him a feeling of completeness and wholeness one more time, while promising to be her knight in shining armor, and maybe she will consent to be his princess.

A week has passed since their sexual encounter, and he is anxious to see her for her tennis lesson tomorrow. The anticipation of standing next to her makes him feel giddy. He will paint what happened in a different light. Gabby was just surprised, that's all. He never meant to hurt her. "I'm sorry," he'll say.

He is beginning to realize that she is different from the numerous other women he has had affairs with. While most women flirt and play up to him, Gabby is more reserved and shy around him. She is wealthy, classy, and smart. Is she out of his league? Brett also realizes that he was totally different when he came on to her. He was so eager to satisfy his own desires that he didn't recognize that she didn't want his advances until he saw that haunting look in her eyes.

He wants her to understand that he made a mistake in thinking she would like his playfulness. He needs her to believe that he is not a monster. He needs to convince her that he is sorry. He wants to be her friend; more accurately, he wants to be her lover. He wants a second chance—a chance to show her that he is a good man. Another go-around with her is his most earnest wish. He can make this right. He can fix it if he can get Gabby to listen.

As his mind drifts to thoughts of her—her walk, the bob of her blond ponytail as she runs to hit a tennis ball, and the flash of her white teeth when she smiles—it makes him grin.

When Gabby's mind drifts to thoughts of Brett, it makes her tremble. She can smell his cologne. She can feel his hands on her skin. Feeling the palpitations of her heart, she fears others can hear and see its quickened and erratic beats. What is wrong with her?

She takes many long hot showers during that week after the rape. When in the shower, she is clean and feels normal. Her mind craves these sensations. However, each time she towel-dries, she brushes the abrasion on her lower back, reminding her of Brett, quickly snatching away the benefits of the shower. The abrasion is only an inch wide and should have a scab by now, but with her desire to be clean, Gabby reopens the wound by scrubbing it obsessively, hating that it is a constant reminder that she cannot erase. She turns, staring at it in the mirror, relieved once again that Richard is out of town. He will be coming back this evening, and with the abrasion still visible, she needs to fabricate some sort of explanation to hide its true origin.

Looking once again into the mirror, she doesn't recognize the frail woman staring back. Mustering all of her courage, she yells, "I'll show him—that arrogant rapist." Her voice finally screams the word that has escaped her for the past few days. The word rings out, bouncing off the walls of her bathroom and back to her listening ears. She doesn't wish to hear the word but hear it she must, or she will never have a chance to heal. The hurt is finally verbalized in its proper context. Brett is a rapist, and she loathes him.

Tears fill her eyes as her legs buckle, and she goes to her knees. Once again, the flood of tears gives her anguish a voice. This time, there is no brush or canvas to transfer her pain. She is alone. Kneeling, she hangs her head, shaking and sobbing. There on her knees, she prays to God to give her strength to face Brett, to take away her pain, and to restore her to her former self.

She begins to see the light in her dark world when she remembers that she is a King. The King family has a history of being a tough breed. It is documented that one of her relatives bravely fought in the great battle of the Alamo. A King is strong. A King is a fighter. Her recent behavior has been everything but strong. Her father is strong, and he is a fighter. What will he think of her weakness? Biting her lip, she is determined not to be a coward. Maybe she has relied on her daddy far too long.

Growing up on the ranch, her life was a complete contrast to what life is offering her today. Gabby misses her carefree life on the ranch. When she was young, her life was simple. She would ride her horse, pick wildflowers from the meadows, and wade through the creek barefoot on many a hot Texas summer day. That little girl of yesteryear had no glimmer of her future life, especially one absent of her mother. She wants to return to those carefree, happy days, even if only for a few hours. She remembers her father working the ranch, right alongside the ranch hands. She vividly remembers the corralling of the longhorns and getting them ready for branding. There are so many happy memories. She just wants to relish all of them. With everything going wrong in her life right now, she wonders if folks ever get a redo, and if they do, will they choose the alternative fork in the road the second time around?

Her family still owns the ranch located west of the town, and Gabby tries to get there at least one weekend a month. Though lately, she has been too busy. When she closes her eyes, she can see it well. The raised ranch house is a tan stucco building with a huge wrap-around wooden porch that is home to a half-dozen rocking chairs. Her mother and dad loved to spend evenings after dinner, sitting in the porch chairs, watching the sun set in the western sky, listening to nature's whispers—the wind that sweeps through the cactus and the living creatures welcoming evening's cooler temperatures. As dusk settled in, they would play a game. All three would search the horizon to see who could spot the first star. Gabby smiles as she recalls her mother counting the stars from that first one sighted until they were too numerous to count.

In the days following the rape, Gabby continues to paint to heal her wounds. She has painted many long hours, but no masterpieces grace her walls. Through her veil of tears, she has taken her brush to the canvases with disappointing results. However, this time when she approaches the easel, she has a plan.

She steps back to view her creation. This time, she nods her head up and down in approval. This time, the canvas doesn't mock her. She holds her hands to her chest and heaves out a deep breath. Her eyes are wide, and she is fascinated with her creation. Before her is a dynamic abstract: the red paint speaks of vitality, the bold strokes depict strength, and the lines show energy. The painting gives her hope. "I am a King. I am strong," she says with confidence. "I will get that necklace back."

Today is her tennis lesson with Brett. She dreads this day but feels he will win again if she caves and is a no-show. She has avoided going outside the condo except to go to Art Smart because she couldn't lie to Rita any longer. Going back to the country club to face her attacker is huge. It takes hours to get herself ready to go to the club. What should she wear? She has always been one to care about her appearance, never going out without a touch of makeup or her long blond hair done just right. Is this sending the wrong message to Brett? She never intended to entice him.

Today, she does not want to wear too much makeup or use her favorite Chanel. Choosing her tennis clothes very carefully, she doesn't wear anything revealing. It is hard to hide a body that most women envy and that causes men to give catcalls. After much thought, she chooses a modest black tennis dress with a rounded neck instead of one of her newer dresses that has thin straps and a built-in bra.

Getting the necklace from Brett cannot happen soon enough. This is the drive behind her current strength, being strong enough to go to the club and approach him. She has a plan.

CHAPTER 4

Gabby patiently waits for everyone to clear before walking onto the court. She can feel the weight of her body as she has to convince her feet to keep moving forward to take another step. Her mind is dreading the outcome of the next few minutes, but she must be brave. *Take some deep breaths. Focus.* Perspiration beads on her bare skin.

With a big sigh she prays, "Please don't let him see me shaking."

She came here with a purpose, and nothing is going to stop her. Reminded of her refusal to live another second with feelings of weakness, she bravely walks with her head held high. She will stand up for herself. *God gave me a voice and I will use it!*

Approaching, she knows Brett cannot escape, and she is so thankful that the adjacent court is empty. Maintaining her secret is her most earnest hope. When she is within arm's length of Brett, she slaps him right on that amazing dimple—she slaps him hard. Never has she envisioned doing such a thing, but her survival instincts take over. She wants to hurt him.

Brett, taken by surprise, grabs her wrist and carefully twists her arm, gingerly holding it behind her back. They stand so close that it makes her terribly uncomfortable. Can he hear her heart's loud and rapid beating? She can smell his spicy odor combined with sweat. Feeling the heat from his body radiating onto her, her mind takes her back to that moment seven days ago. He reaches for her chin, forcing her to peer into his green eyes. A few seconds pass, but it seems like minutes as their eyes lock on each other.

Gabby searches into those deep green seas and is shocked to find a sincerity in Brett's face that she has witnessed only once before in her life. It was a decade ago when outside the door of her mother's hospital room, her father, with that same look, sorrowfully explained the events leading up to the moments before her mother's death.

"I am so sorry," Brett says, using those exact words her father stammered that dark day, and those words will forever be etched into her memory. "I never meant to hurt you. I never meant for it to get so out of hand. Nothing like this has ever happened before. You must believe me." He releases her arm.

Stepping away from him, Gabby feels her body start to shake and quiver, but compose herself she must because she is a King. Regaining her poise, she says in the same matter-of-fact voice that she has heard her father use her entire life, "You are a despicable animal. What you did to me is a criminal act."

She lets out a deep breath, sets her shoulders back, and continues, "Best case scenario, I can get you fired. Worst case, I can tell my father, and you can disappear more quickly than you can ever think is imaginable. Gone ... and really, Brett, ask yourself this question, who will really care?" She throws her arms up in the air and pauses a few seconds before adding, "No one, just like I thought. But I haven't done any of those things. If you ever touch me again, you will disappear."

With her hands on her hips and more confidence in her voice, she continues, "You are so lucky that I am allowing you to keep your job, let alone live another day on this earth, you bastard. If I hear my name mentioned in the same sentence as yours, this is surely what will happen to you. Am I making myself clear? I will not be the center of gossip at this club, understand?"

Catching her breath, she looks up at Brett and misreads the shocked look on his face. "You are so pathetic. Look at you standing there like you're clueless. Are you that arrogant that you think every woman wants you to fuck her? Pathetic!"

"Gabby, listen, I already told you I never intended for it to happen the way it did. I wanted you, and I thought you wanted me. Now, I know I was wrong, but at the time it seemed right."

She turns and starts walking off the court but remembers her main purpose for the confrontation. True, the rape is severe in itself. She is not taking it lightly, but she needs that necklace almost as much as she needs to breathe air for life. Turning back to Brett, who is standing in a stunned trance, she demands, "I want my necklace back, now."

Not waiting for him to reply, she quickly finds her way off the court. Blinded by a flood of tears, she cannot get to the ladies' room fast enough. Hearing his footsteps near, she closes the bathroom door and locks it. She turns her back to the door and muffles her sobs.

"Gabby," he softly pleads. "Please come out. We need to talk."

Her reply is immediate. "Go away, you monster. Go away. Haven't you done enough already? Just go away."

She wipes her tears and sighs in relief that she held her composure. She opens the bathroom door with caution. *Please, let him not be here, please.* There is no exit from the club from the lower level, so she needs to ascend the stairs, taking the chance that Brett or someone else might see her. Stephen, the manager of the club, passes her, but his head is down, reading a document, and Gabby is thankful she doesn't have to fake a smile or force some superficial conversation. After a few hellos to acquaintances along the path to the exit and a goodbye to the receptionist, she is finally out of that toxic environment.

Escaping outside into the warm sunshine, she sucks in a deep breath, filling her lungs with the crisp air. Equally, she exhales and envisions all of the bad leaving her body with that breath. Okay, she has done it. She loads her tennis bag into her Mercedes. She has approached Brett, stated her case, and given him her ultimatums. She has given a voice to the inner thoughts that have been swimming in the oceans of her mind for the past week. It is like finding a life raft. She grabbed on to it, for she is a survivor, and she will conquer this man. She is a King.

Lifting her head high, she realizes the day really is beautiful. She has come here for a workout and work out she will. She decides to go for a run on the nearby trail that encircles the club. The trail was created just a few years ago because members wanted an outdoor opportunity for exercise as a change of pace from the indoor gym with its treadmills and elliptical trainers. One lap is a little less than a mile, and today she feels so much lighter, having the heavy burden of the confrontation with Brett behind. She needs to run and try to get her life back to normal.

Gabby, who has not always been a runner, started running a few years ago out of necessity. There were many rainy days one winter season that prevented playing tennis. There are only a few indoor courts in the whole city, and these are frequently booked a week ahead of time. Unless there is a last-minute cancellation, hopes of booking one of these courts are extremely slim. Exercising indoors does not cut it for Gabby. She is a physical type and desires to be close to nature. So, she started running. It was not easy at first; she would huff and puff after a short distance and would ask herself why folks would torment themselves with this activity. But after a few weeks, she had a change of heart and even enjoyed it. One thing that she did learn was that no matter how many years a person ran, or how many times a week they ran, that first half-mile was always the worst.

At first, running makes her feel awful. It isn't painful, just not a good feeling. Not until she gets her heart and breathing regulated and her muscles warm does she settle into it and, yes, enjoy it. She never does get that "high" that she hears other runners boast about, but she enjoys the exercise and the burning of calories. She loves to eat, but her metabolism has changed and, unlike her younger days, she is no longer able to eat anything she wants, whenever she wants. She still enjoys food but needs to counterbalance her intake with an exercise program that burns lots of calories. Running provides that as well as clearing her mind.

Grabbing her iPod from her car, she turns to the trail. She loves to run to the sound track from the movie, *A Knight's Tale,* and loves the beat of its songs because the rhythm matches the beating of her heart as she runs. What a release exercise is for her. She has pent herself up in her condo for a week and denied herself the chance to feel alive. Her grief and depression have overtaken her entire existence. Now, that is in the past. This is the present. She is a fighter. She is strong. She will survive.

While she runs, the sore at the base of her spine where her skin is broken from the assault and worsened by her obsessive scrubbing is now being rubbed by her tennis shorts. It is one more constant reminder of Brett. She allows her mind to go there—to think of Brett. There had been several times over the course of his employment at the club when she actually did consider him dating material; however, that was before she learned he was a philanderer from listening to the gossip about his promiscuous behavior. Gabby has the mind-set of an old-fashioned girl. Her philosophy is simple when it comes to relationships. As the country-and-western song lyrics go, she is a one-man woman and needs a one-woman man. Brett does not fit that model.

Well, neither does Richard, if she were really honest. About a year into their relationship, a club member saw Richard with another woman on one of his business trips. Gabby had volunteered to accompany Richard, as the trip was over her birthday, but he declined her invitation. When the news came to her a few weeks later, she was hurt but after Richard's pleading, she forgave him. Realizing that she wasn't getting any younger and knowing how much her father liked Richard, she thought it best to give him another chance.

Now, running helps clear her head, causing her to put into perspective the happenings in her world. As she considers all her previous encounters with Brett, there were good times and some flirting, but was there any harm in that? Most women flirt, even the married women. She thinks back to her actions on the court with Brett over the past few months. She also tries to understand that look in his eyes that reminded her so much of her father during the worst time of her life, her mother's death. Brett did try to apologize, and he sincerely looked the part, but even that cannot justify his actions. Trying to remember his exact words is difficult because, at the time, she was so wrapped up in her own outpouring of words, trying to make her threats sound convincing.

"Why can't I remember?" she questions aloud. Then, she does remember Brett saying something about how he never intended to go that far and how things got out of hand.

God, it doesn't make any sense. Would a monster say those things? At the least, maybe she should consider giving him a chance to explain. It really can't make the situation any worse. Besides, she still needs to get her necklace back, and she will get that back from him regardless.

❖❖❖❖❖❖

Brett admitted that things had gotten out of hand, but to be called a rapist—well, that was something new. But then again, this is all new to him. He has never experienced a woman who twisted his imagination and permeated his thoughts as much as this one. Thinking back to that day on the court, he was so overpowered by his emotion and physical desire that he wasn't thinking. He was just reacting. He smiles, remembering how he relished the feeling of power and victory. Never before had he been so complete and whole. However, now that Gabby has cried rape and threatened him, his previous feeling that this time he acted differently is confirmed.

Since he had blocked off time in his schedule for his lesson with Gabby, he finds himself with a free hour. He decides some fresh air is in order, and exercise will be just what he needs. He quickly changes from his tennis Nikes into his running shoes and hits the trail that surrounds the country club. Going for a leisurely jog in the middle of the day is a rare luxury.

Sprinting along, he lets his mind drift to Gabby. It brings a smile to his face to remember the fire in her eyes and the sting of the slap. She is a little tigress and that excites him more. He has always admired her for her womanly curves, but now he admires her spunk. Gabby is a puzzle, and with each day he is learning more about her, trying to fit the pieces together.

The occupation of a tennis professional in a prestigious club has its privileges, and one of those privileges is lending an ear to gossip. When women are together, they get so involved in their conversations that the real reason they gathered is quickly forgotten. Frequently, Brett needs to clear his throat rather loudly, reminding them they are wasting their lesson, as he will be paid regardless. It does not bother him if they prefer to chat rather than learning how to improve their top spin on a backhand or increase the power of their serve. Many times, the women forget that he is even on the court, and he hears gossip that would make the worldliest of the male species blush.

It was several months ago that Gabby was the topic of their outlandish tongue-wagging—or rather, her boyfriend, Richard, to be exact. He had been seen with a petite brunette, and he enjoyed her outward display of public affection. Even though Richard and Gabby are not married, everyone knows they are considered exclusive. During their lesson with Brett, the club members were openly debating whether they should make Gabby aware of Richard's unfaithfulness. These rumors made Brett pay closer attention to the beautiful and wealthy girl.

He secretly delighted in learning this information because he viewed it as a crack in the door. It gave him a glimmer of hope that Gabby might become his someday. This particular incident started his infatuation with her. He visualized her hurt and crying over the broken affair. She would confide in him while taking a lesson. He would be empathetic and listen tenderly as he has played this role so many times before. Then he would make his move and approach her. In her broken state and quick to have revenge, she would have sex with him. He would be viewed as a compassionate friend who cares instead of the guy who wants quick, easy sex with perks. It always worked this way. It was exciting and even romantic at times. *Isn't that what women want*, Brett thinks ... *a little romance, some excitement?*

Jogging along, he becomes aware of the songs of the birds as he comes to the straight part of the trail farthest from the tennis center. He fills his lungs with air and looks up in search of them. There isn't a cloud in the sky. He is feeling much better and then he catches a glimpse of a long blond ponytail in the distance. At first, he thinks his mind is playing tricks on him, but then he realizes that it is not a mirage; it really is Gabby jogging. He increases his pace to a run. He must catch her and explain. Apologize again, if that's what it takes. Quickly, his strides match Gabby's. Shocked to see Brett next to her, she stops dead in her tracks. She has been deep into the music from her iPod and hasn't heard him approach.

"Really," she says disgustedly, yanking the wires from her ears. Reaching down to grab her knees, trying to catch her breath, she looks up into his face. Conscious of his green eyes staring at the cleavage above her sports bra, she quickly stands upright and turns red. Brett laughs, making her all that much more uncomfortable. "You've got some nerve," she mutters.

He reaches out to touch her shoulder. She quickly backs away while shoving his hand with her own. Respectful of this, Brett continues in a burst of short sentences. "Let me explain. I know that I came on too strong. I got carried away. I thought you would be okay with having some fun. I like you, and I thought you liked me, and, well, since Richard ..."

"Since Richard what?" She glares at Brett with a puzzled expression.

He looks down at his feet, as he isn't sure Gabby knows, and it isn't his intention to be the person to pass on gossip; however, it is to his advantage, and he needs everything he can think of to change her perspective of him. He searches her eyes and continues tenderly. "He steps out on you."

He stands looking at the face he has thought about a million times in these past few months. He sees she is uneasy with the subject, but instantly she replies, rebuffing him, "That's none of your concern."

Okay, Brett thinks. *Let her stew over that for a while.* He watches her jog away in the opposite direction.

He is playing his cards carefully, getting out of the mess he created. He is pleased about the confrontation on the jogging trail; he feels it has given him the upper hand. He created a diversion, a great tactic used in warfare. Has he gotten Gabby to turn her anger away from him and focus that anger on her two-timing boyfriend? Maybe her anger against Richard will get her to break off their relationship. Then Richard will be out of her life so Brett can move on in.

Richard is very influential with the locals and makes a lot of money, but even though money can buy many things, money cannot buy love. Brett is sure that Gabby isn't in the relationship with Richard for the money, as she comes from a long line of wealthy Texans who made their money in ranching and drilling the oil under those ranches. He also wants to believe that she is not in love with Richard. Why would she want to be with someone who cheats?

Brett finishes his run and is quite pleased that the situation with Gabby is finally looking a little better in spite of the threats she made on the tennis court. She hasn't reported him and after this much time has passed, he is pretty sure that he is in the clear as far as the law is concerned. Since Richard is an attorney, Brett would be lying if he said the thought of being prosecuted for rape didn't pass through his mind. Plus, if he loses his job, he can get another, but he enjoys his current job and doesn't want the hassle of starting over somewhere else. More importantly, there is Gabby. He is not willing to leave her. Well, not just yet.

After running, he goes back to the tennis club. As he opens his locker to shower, there is Gabby's necklace dangling from the hook. It begs him to caress it and take hold of it. He does, continuing his thoughts of clasping this necklace around Gabby's neck, as she stands naked before him. Lately, it is his one and only daydream. Why has she taken over all of the sexual images that come into his mind? When he tries to conjure up thoughts of other women, his mind always inserts Gabby into his dreams. It seems that taking her so aggressively has turned him on so much that she occupies all his thoughts.

For all of that, he is a little concerned, and this concern scares him because he is a stranger to such feelings. Usually with women, he loves them and leaves them. Easy come, easy go. But this time, it feels so different. When he looks in the mirror, he recognizes the guy standing before him in the physical state, but surely the guy with the emotions and current mentality is a complete stranger.

Looking again at the necklace, he rolls the delicate chain through his fingers, wondering two things; first, why this necklace is so important to its owner and, secondly, why it has quickly become his most prized possession. Sure, it looks as if it were fourteen-karat gold; however, the knot on the end is small and ordinary. It can easily be replaced. But replacing it is not going to be necessary as Brett is going to use this necklace to get time with the one woman who is on his mind constantly. Normally, he places a memento from his affair into a small black box in his locker. His collection has greatly increased since he started working at the country club. In fact, he has even considered whether he should get a second box or just get a bigger one. However, this necklace is not going to find its way into that box as it is going to get him something that he wants more than a memento.

He smiles. *I will call Gabby, arrange for a meeting in a public place, and guarantee that I will give back her necklace. She'll have to meet with me.*

Certainly, that will force her to see him. He kisses the small gold knot and replaces it on the hook, thinking that he has to get the clasp fixed before returning it to Gabby. Looking down, he confirms what he already knows; he is aroused. He will have to wait before walking to the showers. Covering himself with a towel, he sits on the bench and Googles the nearest jewelry store on his phone. He calls and arranges to drop off the necklace, getting it repaired before phoning Gabby. He wants everything to be perfect for that union.

Excited but with some reservation, he stops at the jewelry store on his way home from work. The jeweler is a friendly, elderly man.

"Can I help you?" he asks as Brett enters the store.

"Yes, I need a new clasp on this necklace," Brett says, nervously running his fingers through his hair.

"Let me take a look at what you have there," the jeweler replies, reaching to take the necklace. He looks at the chain and smiles, searching Brett's face. "Yes, that's an easy fix. It will only take a few minutes. If you have the time, I can do it now."

As the old man goes to his desk in the back of the store, Brett looks in the glass cases before him filled with sparkling diamonds and precious metals. How can anyone ever make a lifetime commitment? He just isn't ready to cross that milestone and cannot envision when he will. Why has he never had a serious relationship? The whole idea of marriage is rather foreign, and he is perfectly content to keep it that way. Why are women so desperate to get married? Sure, some of his friends have tied the knot, but it seems that few of them consider themselves happy, and many are divorced and in a second relationship.

Continuing past the engagement and wedding rings, he comes to another case that holds gold chains and earrings beneath the glass, and searches for something similar to the trinity knot that the jeweler is repairing. Not finding anything, he picks up a catalog and starts flipping through its glossy pages. Almost giving up, Brett turns to the back cover, and there is an entire trinity knot collection, which includes a necklace slightly bigger than Gabby's as well as matching earrings and a bracelet. The bracelet seems too complicated as there are two lengths listed. How would a guy know what length to buy? But the pierced earrings, well, there is no size involved there. It would be so easy to buy them for Gabby. Deep in his thoughts, Brett is startled, finding the jeweler standing next to him.

"All finished," the man proclaims, holding the necklace up to the light for him to inspect. "I shined it up for you. Wait here a second. I'll give you a box." The jeweler reaches under the counter, retrieving a small velvet box.

Shyly, Brett says, "These earrings," pointing to the back page of the sales brochure. "They match this necklace. Do you carry them?"

"No, but I can order them for you. They should be here in three days using express delivery if you need them fast."

Seconds later, Brett is handing the man his credit card and filling out the form for express delivery.

Once behind the wheel of his car in the parking lot, he hesitates before starting his car and picks up his phone. He knows he needs to dial the number quickly before losing his nerve. Gabby may not even take his call, but he has to try.

When he hears her pick up on the other end, quickly he says in a less than confident voice, "Hello, Gabby, this is Brett."

He listens, anticipating a click discontinuing the call, but there is only silence. He continues very cautiously.

"I know my actions were inappropriate and you're upset. You asked for your necklace back. Can we meet at the coffee shop?" He holds his breath, waiting for her answer. Again, there is silence, making him nervous, but he just waits.

Finally, he is forced to ask again, "Gabby, you there?" A few more seconds pass in silence. Now, he is not sure what to do. However, the call is not disconnected, so he holds on the line, waits, and prays to hear her voice.

Gabby finally weakly answers, "Yes, I'm here. No, I can't. I'm terribly busy."

He is disappointed. It has taken all of his nerve to dial her number. After hanging up, he thinks, *Okay, on to plan B. Where there is a will, there is a way.* He opens the box with the necklace and takes it out, admiring its luster, and thinks of Gabby. How she will react when he clasps the trinity knot around her neck.

Using his iPhone to connect to the web, he types in the name of the local art gallery, knowing that Gabby works there during the week. He scrolls through the website to find its opening hours. He also sees information for Gabby's art exhibition and reception to be held next month. The name of her art exhibition is the Trinity Knot Series.

This title intrigues him. *First, she has a trinity knot necklace and now, she's painted a series.* He needs to find out the connection between the knot and the girl. Remembering his initial motivation for the call, he comes to believe that maybe Gabby really is busy. His hopes of meeting with her are once again revived as he devises a new plan. Thinking cleverly, a spontaneous smile creeps over his face.

I will drop the necklace off at her work, he thinks, scratching his chin.

Her refusal to meet him at the coffee shop may be a blessing in disguise as it will force them to meet at her art gallery. His arrival at the gallery will take her by surprise, another great tactic used in warfare. There is no doubt in his mind that he will win this game. He feels he has gained control once again in pursuing this relationship and is confident that he can convince her to give him another chance. Nurturing the fire that stirs deep inside, he is certain that he can stoke that same fire of desire in Gabby. He has seen it in her eyes, and he felt it over these last few months. Remembering his seduction of her at the tennis center, he is concerned that he may lose control again, and this power that struggles inside still holds a grip on him. He needs to be cautious.

<hr />

Sitting at the tennis desk, Brett is relieving the receptionist over the lunch hour. He is enjoying the quiet as no one is in the shop and the phone is silent. Getting a break from the Texas sun is also an added benefit of filling in at the desk, and he is able to check his e-mails and return voice messages. Distracted from his duties by a faint noise, he finds Gabby standing at the corner of the desk.

"Hello, Gabby," he says cheerfully.

Meeting his stare, Gabby's eyes open wide. She quickly turns away and bolts down the hallway. He jumps out of his chair, rounds the desk, yelling after her, "Wait, Gabby. Let's talk."

It's too late; she is already out of sight, but he is sure she was able to hear his plea. He saw her haunted stare. It is confirmation that his apology was not accepted. Does she hate him? Does she still think him a rapist? Thinking back to that day on the court, he is reminded of the feeling of power and victory. Why did he behave that way? Was it the sex or the power that caused him to act so aggressively? Now he knows his fantasies were inadequate. For years, he has fooled himself, believing the sexual acts are the attraction. No, it is the power. Gabby's eyes haunt him, sending him a clear message that he has been telling himself a lie. It was her look of utter defeat. He knows this feeling, and he vows never again.

CHAPTER 5

Having eaten dinner more than an hour ago, Gabby sits at the table in their condo waiting for Richard. She came home from work early to make one of his favorite dishes. She got the recipe from his mother and wants to surprise him with meat-stuffed cabbage rolls smothered in a marinara that will knock your socks off. She has set the table in her mother's pink rose china. As a child, Gabby loved seeing these dishes on the table because it meant a celebration with laughter, great food, and plenty of it. To this day, the pink rose is still her favorite flower and tonight, she wants an evening with laughter and happiness.

It is the two-year anniversary of Gabby and Richard's first date. She is sure that Richard hasn't the slightest clue. He never pays much attention to dates on the calendar other than his court dates. He is late again, but that's nothing unusual; it seems to be happening more frequently. What will his excuse be this time? She understands the value of hard work and putting in long hours to get ahead. Richard's drive to be successful is one of the characteristics that drew her to him. When he phoned earlier, he mentioned leaving the office but something must have come up. How can she blame him if she chose not to remind him of their anniversary? She wanted the celebration to be a surprise.

Alas, the surprise is on her. She lets the candle burn low as she sips her chardonnay. She sits in the dim romantic light, closes her eyes, and listens to the soft music. Here, in this quiet place, alone, she questions her relationship. What does Richard mean to her? Does she love him? What does she mean to him? Does he love her? So many questions to ponder, and tonight, she has plenty of time to think about those answers. She knows Richard has had at least two affairs during these two years. Are there more?

What attracted her to Richard initially, besides his good looks, was his sharp, persuasive wit. She thought him a prize catch, but he cannot be trusted, and his infidelity has taken a major toll on their relationship. Richard uses his persuasive wit to lure women into his bed. Why did he want them to live together if he wasn't committed to an exclusive relationship?

In the beginning, she forgave him for his affair and accepted his apology along with a promise that it would never happen again, but then it did happen again, just a few months ago. If Brett knows about the affairs, Richard's infidelity is more well-known in the community than she ever dreamed. Why is she staying in this relationship with a man she cannot trust? Doesn't she deserve better?

The next morning, she crawls out of bed early to get her shower before her tennis match. She does not want to disturb Richard. She can hear his rhythmic, even breathing and knows he is in a deep sleep. She had hit the sack around midnight. A light sleeper, she wears earplugs to bed because the slightest click of the ceiling fan or noise in the parking lot below will awaken her. So, she has no idea what time Richard finally came home. She lingers in the shower, feeling the warm water splash over her tanned body.

Now, while she stands in a towel at her vanity, combing her hair, Richard sneaks up behind her, startling her, as he drops her towel to the floor and wraps his arms around her. Cupping her breasts with both hands, he kisses her neck.

"Good morning," he whispers softly into her ear. "You smell nice." With that, he leans her over the counter, parts her legs, and presses himself into her from behind. His hands grab her buttocks as he pumps into her. Gabby closes her eyes and tries to close off her mind.

She holds her breath and prays that the tears in her eyes do not fall down her cheeks. Richard, so involved in satisfying his own desires, is unaware of the wet drop that splashes onto the counter. It isn't that he doesn't care about Gabby, but meeting his own needs trumps any issue that she may be having. After his orgasm, he finds the scab on her lower back and brushes the edges of it lightly with his finger.

"Hey, what's this?" he asks, examining her back more closely.

"Just something crazy that I did," she lies, wiping her face. "You know how clumsy I am and always bumping into things."

"It looks like a carpet burn from some rough sex. Back in my college days, my girlfriend would have those when we screwed around on the carpet for lack of a bed. Who are you screwing? I've been out of town, so who's the lucky guy?" Richard asks jokingly.

Taken aback by his question and irritated by his joke, Gabby turns around and sarcastically quips, "Who am I screwing? Really, do you expect me to answer that?"

Taking a step back, Richard quickly adds, "Hey, just kidding. Geez, someone got up on the wrong side of the bed."

Changing the subject and grateful that he doesn't notice her tears, she questions, "Hey, what time did you get in last night, or should I say early this morning?"

She knows that she has to play the aggressor and turn the attention of this conversation away from herself and put Richard on the defensive. She is shaken that he has seen her abrasion. She is never good at thinking fast on her feet, and if she fumbles in the least, Richard will be sure to pick up on her insecurity. It is his job to know people and read their body language, matching it with the emotion in their voice. He has a sixth sense and is rarely wrong.

She has made the decision not to report Brett and not to tell anyone, including Richard and Ella. If Richard knows, he will go to his friends at the police station and make her file a report. She wants to forget about the rape, not talk about it. It's a small town, and the gossip will be unbearable. She wonders how Richard will react if he does find out. Will his feelings for her change? After hearing the entire story, will he blame her? These are questions that she wants to leave unanswered.

Continuing her offensive attack, she adds, "I tried calling your cell last night, but it went straight to voice mail. I left you several messages—did you get them?" Not waiting for an answer, she continues, "Yesterday was our anniversary. I made you a special dinner: candles, music, china, and your favorite stuffed cabbage rolls. You missed it. Where were you?"

He takes her in his arms and rocks her. She cannot hold her tears from him any longer. She cries. He believes her tears are from him missing dinner last evening. "I am so sorry. I had to work. You know I can't take phone calls when I'm with clients. It's a busy time of the year for me. A lawyer works long hours—well, if he wants to be successful. You want that for me, right? For us?" Holding her, he kisses her on the forehead. "Am I forgiven?"

She nods, sniffles, and leans into Richard more closely.

"I promise I'll make it up to you," he says. "I'll take you out to dinner tonight, okay? Just you and me. You pick the place. Just let me know the time and I will be there. I swear."

CHAPTER 6

G abby is glad to step into the air-conditioned gallery, getting
out of the Texas sun. She can feel the heat from the scorching
parking lot permeate through the soles of her sandals.
Grateful to cross over the threshold into the gallery, she hears Rita's
laughter ringing out, causing her to smile. She loves Rita and is glad to
have her in her life. As she rounds the corner, following the direction
of the voices, she is stunned to find Brett sitting on the couch having
tea with Rita. The mere sight of him stops Gabby in her tracks. Her
stomach drops. *Why is Brett at the store?*

Rita glances up, patting the couch and motioning Gabby to join
them. Reluctantly, Gabby sits down next to Rita, wiping the sweat
from her forehead, staring at Brett.

"Hello, Gabby," Brett chirps cheerfully. "Rita was just telling me about your show and invited me to your reception. I would be delighted to attend."

Gabby quickly interjects without giving him a chance to go on. "I didn't think that art would be your thing. Not enough action. I am sure an evening here at the gallery will be terribly boring for you." She wants him to go away. *I am giving you a free pass. Please take it.*

"Nonsense," he chimes. "I will be honored to attend. You never know, I can become one of your biggest fans." Then glancing back at Rita, he adds, "I am so grateful that this charming woman has given me so much of her time. It has been a pleasure meeting you, but I really do need to get to work."

Standing quickly, he reaches into his pocket and pulls out a small box. He opens the lid, showing Gabby its contents.

"My necklace," she gasps, quickly getting up from the couch.

Taking the necklace into his strong hands, he explains, "I hope you don't mind that I took the liberty to have it repaired. Let me help you put it on."

Feeling very awkward, she doesn't know how to decline his offer, and she can see Rita's eyes dancing with delight. She turns, offering her back to Brett as he takes the necklace out of the box. He closes the gap between them, pushing her long hair to one side. She can smell his spicy scent and feel his soft, warm breath on her neck, and she prays that he doesn't see the goose bumps rising on her arms. Due to the heat, she has chosen a thin silk shell with small straps, exposing just a touch of her cleavage, leaving plenty of her bare skin for him to admire and touch. She feels his warm hands touch her neck and shoulders, lingering a few seconds before he closes the clasp, fastening the necklace securely. Moving his hands to her shoulders, he pivots her around to face him.

"Let's see how it looks," he says. He lifts her chin, as he did that time before behind the curtain, so their eyes can meet. "Beautiful," he remarks, clearly not even making any effort to look at the trinity knot necklace; his stare stays fixed on Gabby's face. "Perfect," he adds in a whisper, so she knows that the word is meant for her ears alone and not for Rita, who is seated on the couch a few feet away.

Gabby can feel the heat creep into her face. Embarrassed, she pulls away and brings her hand to her neck, clasping the trinity knot in her familiar way, sliding it along the chain, back and forth. Glad to have it returned, she looks down at her feet, murmuring, "Thank you," in as loud a voice as she can muster. Backing away, Brett quickly says his goodbyes and walks out the door, grinning.

Rita laughs aloud as soon as the door closes and then starts whistling. "Nice," she says. "Where have you been hiding that hunk ... those muscles, that tan, those brown curls, and those deep green eyes?"

Rita is fanning herself as if she would most certainly faint otherwise. "Not only is he drop-dead gorgeous, but he has the hots for you, little one. And from your flustered reaction, the feeling seems mutual." She reaches out and takes Gabby's hand in her own. "I can't wait to hear how he got your necklace, and more importantly, how it got broken."

"Long story," replies Gabby, touching her necklace for reassurance and courage. Trying to regain her composure, she inhales and lets out a long, slow breath. Not willing to disclose any more information, she turns and walks into the back room, leaving Rita with her mouth hanging open.

He does look great, Gabby finds herself thinking later that night. Brett has that glowing tan from spending hours in the sun and his hair is lightened on the ends. His muscles are ripped. In addition to the hours he is swinging a tennis racquet and running around the court, she sees him frequently in the exercise rooms at the club, lifting weights and running on the treadmill. It's obvious that Brett takes pride in his appearance.

Gabby feels her stomach churn as she anticipates going to the tennis court the following day. She will join her team in a tennis drill with none other than Brett as her coach. She tried to discourage her friends from hiring him for their drills, giving multiple reasons, but the team would have none of it. They teased that if they were spending their money, they wanted the added benefit of feasting their eyes on some candy while improving their game. Gabby does not wish to protest too much even though she has reservations about being on the court with Brett. She has to go along with their decision; however, she knows she should never be caught alone with him. She'll be alert and prepared to defend herself.

As the weeks progress, the team lessons go smoothly. Gabby is reserved around Brett, and he keeps his distance. It seems at times he makes a conscious effort not to even glance her way. What does he want? Is he being aloof because he has moved on, or is he trying to make her feel more comfortable around him? Maybe this whole ordeal is part of some sick game. She is not into playing games—she was suckered into this one, and her intuition is that this is not a game she should be playing. Whatever his motivations are, she is sure not to ask, though it does bother her that she finds herself stealing glances at him and watching his behavior with her teammates. She sees them smiling at Brett and a flow of conversation usually follows. He fascinates her. She studies his mannerisms, and she watches the women's behavior when they are addressing him.

On the court, Ella flirts with Brett more than the other girls in the drill do. Gabby notices how Ella stands close to him and touches him at every possible opportunity. Of course, he enjoys being the center of attention and flirts right back. Gabby just shakes her head. She wonders if she should have a talk with Ella, give her a warning that she should be on her guard when it comes to Brett. She will have to do this without giving any hints of her own personal sexual encounter. She is uncertain what Ella would do with the information if she ever got even a whiff of any wrongdoing. Probably Ella would go right to Richard, and that is something Gabby does not want to chance.

At the end of the lesson as the girls pack their racquets, Ella stands close to Brett and touches his arm. "We should go out sometime," she teases. Then she adds, "I'll make sure you have fun."

Gabby shakes her head in disbelief. Is she more disgusted with Ella or with Brett?

"Maybe we should," replies Brett as he glances in Gabby's direction.

"How about next Friday night?" Ella continues. "You free?"

Brett, his dimple more prominent, smiles. "For you, Ella, I'll make sure I'm free."

Ella beams from ear to ear.

Gabby is flustered. She shakes her head and rolls her eyes. Why does Ella want to date that arrogant playboy? Should Gabby warn her best friend?

She is relieved that the lessons go on without incident as she does not want her team members, who are also her closest friends, to suspect anything. As good-hearted as these girls are, it is difficult to do rumor control. Once someone gets a shred of truth, before long, the whole gang—plus others—will join in, unintentionally distorting everything so badly that it would even be considered funny if no one was being hurt by their gossip.

CHAPTER 7

Today is the day. Since Gabby left the New York art scene and moved back to Texas, she has dreamed of a solo opening at Art Smart. Shortly after hiring her, Rita had handed her the gallery's two-year appointment calendar and told her to pick an open month, setting the dates from hang to strike for her show. Gabby has worked intermittently on her Knot series of acrylic paintings since the death of her mother ten years before. Even though Rita allows her to paint during her working hours at the store, she never works on her Knot series. She paints these only in private at home.

She doesn't even like to work on them in front of Richard, hastily putting them away when she hears his key click in the lock. She believes Richard thinks her abrupt stopping is because he is her entire world, and she is just keeping herself busy until he arrives home from work. However, that is far from the truth. Needless to say, exhibiting this series in the gallery for others to view makes Gabby extremely anxious. These paintings are so close to her heart that the thought of others viewing them makes her envision herself standing emotionally naked before strangers.

Breathing deeply, she has to remind herself with each exhale that she is strong and brave and needs to do this. She is doing this for herself, but also she is doing this for her mother. Closing her eyes, she pictures her mother standing in the gallery, smiling at her work and nodding in approval. Her mother would be so proud of her. Fighting back the tears, she takes some more deep breaths and whispers, "This is for you, Mom." She sighs, adding, "I wish you were here."

At a glance, her artwork seems rather new age, rich in color with distorted views. The colors are high key with deep shades of blues, purples, and golds. She ponders whether she should disclose their true meaning and inspiration. There are two theories relating to artwork: one is for the artist to explain the interpretation, and the second is to allow the work to speak for itself. Gabby has chosen the latter as it will be too emotionally draining for her to describe the intricate layers of meaning that gave birth to each painting. However, she also realizes that by making the decision to withhold their meaning, the paintings may be trivialized, but this is a career risk that she is willing to take.

Of all of her knot paintings, the most sacred to Gabby are the few that show images of her trinity knot from different views and with the light striking from various angles. None of her paintings is overly large. She purposely limits their size, so she can easily transport them in her Mercedes SUV. Experience has taught her that a four-foot-by-five-foot canvas is her limit. Early in her career, she made a large abstract painting and needed to hire a truck and driver to get the painting to the buyer, thus eating away most of her profit. It was a good, quick lesson, and if she has hopes of supporting herself with her art career, she needs to be wiser.

Out of the two dozen paintings, one is a bit more special to her than all the rest. It is a three-by-three square with a bold, single trinity knot in dramatic, brilliant colors. She chose the colors for the painting very carefully and with purpose, using the same colors that are told in a myth about Iris, the Greek Goddess of the Rainbow. The knot is painted in gold with iridescent hues of purple and blue, creating an illusion of light radiating from within. The background is in a deeper purple with undertones of green bursting forth around the knot.

According to the myth, purple is the color representing honor, as Gabby honored and adored her mother, while the blue stands for truth. She could tell her mother anything and everything, and her mother never judged her. That, of course, did not always mean that her mother approved of everything she did, but she listened intently and gave her opinion when it was warranted. The background of the painting represents the darkness that Gabby was engulfed in while struggling to make sense of her loss. Finally, and most importantly, the bursts of green represent healing.

She considers putting a Not for Sale sign on the painting, but she thinks that wouldn't be fair to Rita, and Rita has been nothing short of kind to her. If the painting sells, it will be a good commission for the gallery as it is the most expensive painting in the Trinity Knot Series, and with the economy in such an up-and-down swing, the store is hurting financially. The last thing Gabby wants to see is its closing. If her artwork can make a difference, she is willing to put everything on the line.

That evening, after the gallery closes, she hangs her paintings on the pristine white walls with Rita's help. It doesn't take Rita more than a few seconds to understand that these paintings are not only different in style from Gabby's art that hangs daily, but Gabby also acts differently around them. She is more reserved and quiet as if in deep introspection. Hanging the paintings takes longer than either of them anticipates, and the stars are well-visible in the night sky when they lock the doors and hug.

"Gabby, talk to me," pleads Rita. "What's going on in that little head? You should be so happy. Tomorrow is your opening reception. It is something that you have looked forward to for the past two years." She takes Gabby's hands in her own, looking into her eyes. "Forget about New York. I know you were disappointed that it didn't turn out as you had hoped. You will get another chance. Believe me, you are so young, and you have your whole life ahead of you. It will happen, sweetie. Just be patient."

Patting Gabby on the shoulder and turning her around, Rita then gives her a big motherly hug. Gabby is grateful for her kind words, and she sighs in relief as she takes another sip from the glass of champagne. Prior to hanging her show, Rita brought out the bubbly, popped the cork and toasted to a successful opening.

Over the course of their relationship, Gabby has shared tidbits of her life with her boss. In addition to telling of her love of painting, she also shared stories about her mother and Richard. Feeling the effects of the champagne, she feels secure in sharing her current relationship struggles. She replies wearily, "It's not the art, Rita. I'm sorry to be so down. You're right. Tomorrow should be a happy day. It's Richard."

Even though Rita does not utter a sound, Gabby can read her expression clearly. Rita has that "what did he do now" look as she rolls her eyes. This small gesture is all it takes for Gabby, who has missed those long girl chats with her mother, to break down in tears.

Rita smoothes her hair, encouraging her to cry. She embraces her, remarking, "A good cry is wonderful for the soul."

Through sobs, Gabby tells her of Richard's unfaithfulness and how it has put a wedge between them, and that her feelings toward Richard cannot close that gaping hole.

After listening very intently, Rita looks into her eyes and asks, "But do you love him?"

No response comes out of Gabby's mouth for a few seconds but then a very quiet, "I'm not sure anymore. I have my doubts." Gabby stands there, shocked at her admission. She has worked so hard on her relationship that she has never realized the love she once felt for Richard has evaporated. Is she using her relationship with him to replace the loss of her mother?

"Well, that makes it pretty clear. He's not the one for you, honey," Rita tenderly says. "Move on. Breakups are always painful, but staying in a loveless relationship is even more painful." Then she adds, "Hey, get a good night's sleep. Forget about Richard. Worry about him another day. Tonight, I want you to dream of your success and the journey you have as an artist. Tomorrow will be an awesome day."

Reaching her car, Gabby looks up into the starlit sky. She often gazes upward, hoping to catch a falling star so she can make a wish.

She realizes that others believe this action quite foolish. But this does not stop her from looking up into the vastness. She wonders when her love for Richard vanished. These past few months, it is true that her thoughts have taken her into another man's arms. After the rape, she loathed Brett. Now, after his numerous apologies, though, including sending flowers, having her necklace repaired, and giving it back to her in such a tender way, he is growing on her.

She smiles as she remembers his green eyes. *Brett really is a handsome guy.* Whenever he touches her, she feels the electricity, her skin tingles, and her heart pounds. Why does his touch have such an impact on her? Just two days ago, she allowed him to walk her to her car when leaving the tennis club. *He thinks we had casual sex. Doesn't he realize his fast, aggressive act was rape? Am I crazy to have feelings for this guy?*

Sometimes as she lies awake at night, she remembers how her skin felt beneath Brett's touch, and it doesn't repulse her. Instead, it excites her. *How can this be?* Lately, when Richard makes love to her, it is not his face she sees when she closes her eyes. Brett's smile dances behind her eyelids. Is she crazy?

She catches herself thinking of Brett more and more. Lying awake in bed, she thinks of him, touching herself. In her fantasies, she willingly gives herself over to him. In the future, if the opportunity ever arises, how will she react to his advances? The trauma of that day behind the curtain has faded into what she fears is the Stockholm syndrome. Is she falling for her abuser? Surely, this is not a good thing; however, thoughts of Brett continue to bring a smile to her face.

Gabby is restless and has barely slept. She is reminded of her childhood when she would anxiously wait for Christmas day. She would have trouble sleeping, not wanting to miss Santa's arrival and the joy of waking, rushing to the tree, finding gifts beautifully wrapped beneath. This day is like an adult Christmas, filled with the same anticipation and excitement. Rita has given her the entire day off so she can sleep in and leisurely prepare for her opening reception.

As always on awakening, she throws her hands above her head, sending a phrase of gratefulness and appreciation into the universe. Today is going to be wonderful, and she is ready to embrace it completely. If her mother's death taught her anything, it is that life is a precious gift, and each moment needs to be savored, for living in the present is life's greatest reward. She has worked hard, pouring her grief over the loss of her mother into her paintings, and today is her day for celebration. It's a celebration not only of her evolving art career but also of coming to terms with her mother's death, of being able to celebrate all of the joyous, even sacred moments they had shared in the bond of the mother-daughter relationship. This day was years in the making, and it is going to be wonderful.

Richard has already left for the office hours before, so she has the condo to herself. She pulls the curtain open and sees that the sun is just peeking through the branches of the oak tree. Peering up into the blue sky dotted with tiny white puffs, she thinks it is indeed going to be a wonderful day.

Suddenly, her thoughts are interrupted by the ringing of her cell phone. Picking it up from her bedside stand, she hears her father's boisterous voice proclaim, "Good morning, darlin'," in his western twang. "Hope I didn't wake you. I know it's early for a princess, but I couldn't wait any longer." Not giving Gabby any time even to attempt to break his speech, he goes on with a hint of urgency. "I'm having flowers delivered to the gallery, pink roses, your favorite. Rita knows to expect them. Get yourself all dolled up, and I will see you tonight. Looking forward to it."

Finally, there is a pause for her to jump into the conversation. "Good morning to you, Daddy. Yes, I was up. Who can sleep in on a day like today? Thanks for the flowers."

"Just an excuse to talk to Rita. Gotta go, my love," he says. The thought of her father and Rita together brings a smile to her face. However, her father is such a tease; it is always hard to decipher his true feelings. "See you tonight," are his final words, followed by a click and just like that, he is gone.

Gabby loves her father, and she knows she is his whole world since her mother passed. He is the main reason she moved back to Texas. Even though he never said it, she could hear the loneliness in his voice. Both of them miss her mother. As far as family, they only have each other. With this thought, she brings her trinity knot necklace to her lips and kisses it, glancing out the window, looking up at the sky, wishing once more that her mother could attend her reception. Her mother had always encouraged her to draw and paint for as long as she can remember. Her mother would be so proud. This, Gabby knows in her heart.

After a leisurely lunch while still in her pajamas, her doorbell rings.

She is embarrassed to answer looking as she does—pj's, no makeup. *Oh, well.* She opens her door. There is no one there, but a large box rests on her step. It is wrapped in shiny gold paper with a huge pink bow. After examining the box for a label or something to distinguish who sent it, finding nothing, she presumes that the present is from her father. She shakes her head, smiling. *So that is why he called.*

She quickly gathers the box inside and starts to shake it—a habit she loves to do with any present, trying to guess what treasure is waiting within. Surprisingly, the box isn't very heavy for its size. She doesn't have a clue what can be hiding inside, so she starts removing the shiny paper with a few quick tears. Saving the pink ribbon, she drapes it over the corner of one of her paintings hanging on the wall. Inside the box is a smaller velvet box.

She is getting more excited as she loves jewelry. Her fingers quickly go to work untying the small pink ribbon that adorns the velvet box. Opening the lid, she gasps at the trinity knot earrings. *How very thoughtful.* He thinks of everything. She holds the earrings up to her ears, admiring them in her mirror. They are gold and just a bit smaller than the knot on her necklace. She instantly loves them. They are the perfect companion to her necklace. She makes a mental note to remember to thank her father, as she does not want to forget in her excitement at the reception.

After applying her favorite Chanel, she gives herself the critical eye in the full-length mirror. Her off-white pantsuit is very classy, the jacket covering a gold lamé shell with thin spaghetti straps. High-heeled gold sandals adorn her feet. Previously, she had a full mental debate over the selection of the shoes, but the importance of being eye-level with her guests won over comfort. Experience tells her that more paintings are bought by men than women. Whether they buy the paintings for their wives or lovers or for their businesses, Gabby wants to be their equal, so adding four inches to her already five-seven frame gives her that subtle advantage. Careful not to be too tall, she also needs to relate to the businesswomen in the crowd. There are so many details for the perfect marketing package, she wonders if most folks even get it.

Gabby is already anticipating the pain from standing for hours in these heeled shoes. Pleased with the reflection staring back at her, she lifts her blond hair, revealing the earrings. Discouraged that they are not noticeable, she decides at the last minute to pin her hair in a loose coil. After making this change, she stands in front of the mirror one last time, fully approving of her look. The earrings, now clearly visible, complement her necklace. She briefly touches the necklace, saying a prayer for a successful opening. Instantly, a feeling of warmth descends upon her as she feels her mother's soft presence. She murmurs, "Thank you," and smiles. Grateful for her mother's approval, she is ready.

The evening at the gallery progresses as planned. Gabby is pleased with the number of guests and the number of sales. The gallery has its own followers who attend, in addition to the invitations that Gabby personally sent to business partners of her father and Richard, and also the members of the country club. The music seems to be the perfect dance partner for the pink roses her father sent that are standing tall on the glass table in the center of the gallery. Her paintings cover the walls, and the guests seem to show genuine interest in them. Some guests actually talk in small groups, discussing color, composition, and lighting.

At first, she is nervous, but later she finds herself enjoying the reception. Relieved no one has asked her to explain her motivation for her artwork, she gives a brief toast. She raises her glass. "Thank you all for coming out tonight and supporting my art." She reaches for Rita and places her arm around her shoulders. "I also want to thank Rita for giving me this opportunity. Rita, you're the best."

The evening is going as well as anyone can hope. There are no surprises.

"Your earrings are perfect. Do you like them?" Brett asks Gabby, raising his glass. He smiles. She is caught off guard.

Oh, my God! In her wildest dreams, she has never imagined they were a gift from Brett. *How embarrassing. He must think me an idiot.*

Without giving her a chance to recover from the shock, he states, "You are so beautiful and talented. Is there anything you cannot do?"

He reaches out to touch an earring, but Gabby pulls away, making an excuse that she has to speak with one of her clients. She needs to put distance between herself and Brett. Over the course of the past few months, even though their conversations have been easier, their relationship has become more complicated. She cannot even fathom how that can be possible. Not after everything that they went through.

Turning to escape, Gabby stops abruptly as Ella is standing right behind her. "My, my, what did I miss?" Ella asks teasingly. She waits for Gabby to answer.

"Nothing, you silly girl. He's all yours." Quickly Gabby makes her escape and rejoins the rest of her guests.

Ella claims Brett by lacing her arm through his. Stealing a glance back at the couple, Gabby is astonished when a small wave of jealousy flows through her. So silly. What is even sillier was her assumption the earrings were a gift from her father. How could she make that mistake?

She thinks all her guests are gone. She is pleased with the way the reception has progressed. Clients and friends came to the reception at a steady pace instead of flooding the gallery all at once. This gave her ample time to spend with each one. She and Rita are both happy because Gabby sold several of her paintings. Did these businessmen buy a painting as a favor to her father? Did Richard make a similar request to his business acquaintances as well? Regardless, a sale is a sale. Pleased that everything went well and no one has really asked her to explain her subject matter, she can barely wait to get out of her high-heeled shoes.

Rita heads for the door, saying, "Gabby, you don't mind cleaning up, do you, dear? I'm really tired. Thanks. Good night."

Winking at Brett, Rita closes the door, leaving against Gabby's protests.

Annoyed at Rita for leaving her alone with Brett, who she thought had already left, Gabby walks over to the couch. "Wow! What a night! My feet are killing me," she says. Taking off her shoes, she looks up at Brett. "Why are you still here? Shouldn't you be with your fans? Ella said everyone was going to the bar at the end of the shopping center."

He motions toward the dirty glasses. "Rita asked you to clean up. I thought I would help." He takes a seat next to her, swinging her feet up on his lap.

Her mouth drops open. "What are you doing?"

"Just helping you. I'm good at this," he offers.

Gabby quips, "You think you are—"

"Come on, Gabby. I said I was sorry. What more do you want from me?"

Reminded of the earrings, she reaches up to touch them. Brett winks, and his smile deepens his dimple. She starts to protest once more, but she is tired and his firm hands on her feet and lower legs feel great. She tries to talk, but he holds his forefinger to his lips, signaling her to be silent. *Okay, I can do quiet,* she thinks.

She closes her eyes and loses herself in the music playing overhead. With the combination of the soft music, the effects of the alcohol, the massage, and the success of the event, Gabby feels excitement stirring between her legs. It has been several weeks since she and Richard have had sex, and now Brett is stroking her. She is breathing harder, and her heart is beating just a bit faster.

When the realization of the situation invades her conscious thoughts, she abruptly sits up, scolding herself for even entertaining thoughts of intimacy with Brett. How can she allow him to touch her? How can she fantasize about how easy it will be to lie here and allow him to massage her, touch her, lavish her body with sweet, wet kisses … and have sex? He raped her. Is she crazy?

"I meant what I said earlier, you are so beautiful," he repeats. Gazing for a split second, he makes another move as if trying to analyze the playing field and steals a light, playful kiss on her cheek.

She has no chance to debate his actions because Richard walks through the gallery door. Quickly standing up, within seconds, Brett is face to face with Richard, each one posturing, waiting for the other to start speaking. Seconds pass. Still, no one speaks.

For Gabby, this silence seems like an eternity. She brushes her hair back and tries to assess from Richard's demeanor if he saw them kiss. Thinking logically, which is a difficult feat for her as her heart is racing, she knows the couch is behind the wall and not visible from the door, so she feels confident that he did not. "Richard, did you forget something?" she inquires.

"Only you," he says, his eyes glaring, dancing from her to Brett, trying to read their expressions.

Play it cool, she tells herself and prays that Brett will do the same. Hopefully, Richard will not notice that she is barefoot and her hair is no longer in the clip. The night was great and not to be ruined by a jealous fight involving two strong personalities and testosterone.

"I thought you might need some help, so I turned around and came back, but I see that your tennis coach has decided to make himself available. How very thoughtful," Richard says, pointing to Brett.

Quickly Brett jumps to Gabby's defense. "I was just leaving," he stammers, then calmly proceeds. "Gabby and I were finishing the final details on the purchase of her painting for my apartment."

Richard continues jokingly, "If you can afford to buy one of Gabby's masterpieces, we are clearly paying too much for our membership at the club."

Ouch, that's just like Richard, Gabby thinks.

Allowing the underhanded remark to slide, Brett turns and shakes Gabby's hand. "Thanks again, Gabby, for a wonderful evening. Good night, Richard." He excuses himself, and turning the corner, he goes out into the night cursing.

Richard's face is red as he fires questions. He grabs her, pulling her arm so she must face him. "What was that all about?"

"Nothing," Gabby responds. *Maybe I responded too quickly. It may come across as being defensive.*

Richard presses her for more. "Nothing," he repeats. "It didn't look that way to me."

"Don't be ridiculous," she says, using a forced casual voice. *Play it cool.*

"You are encouraging him," Richard continues firmly.

She raises her voice. "Oh, no, Richard. You are not going to put me in the jury box of your private courtroom, especially not with you as both the jury and judge." She continues, "Richard, I'm tired. My feet are killing me. My evening was perfect. Let's not change that, okay?"

She decides to leave the cleanup for the morning. She hides her hair clip in her pocket and gathers her shoes. Standing barefoot, she motions Richard toward the door with the key in her hand.

Glad to be out in the night air, she looks up to the stars. What if Richard hadn't come back? Would she and Brett have continued past that first kiss? She hasn't been that aroused by a man in a long time, and even though it feels naughty, it feels good.

She replays the day behind the curtain when Brett made his advances and raped her. At times, she blames herself. She must have sent signals to make him believe that she wanted her. She keeps playing the reel over and over in her mind. As painful as the experience was, it has started to ease over time. Brett has never again exposed that side of him, but it does cause her concern. Well, that is an understatement; it causes a big concern. *Is Brett a Dr. Jekyll and Mr. Hyde? How dangerous is he? What triggers his aggression?*

She remembers an episode on a daytime talk show that explained how women are interested in the bad boys. *Am I one of those women and is Brett one of those boys?* She needs answers. Over the past few months, Brett has been nothing but sweet. Now, there is the issue of the earrings he bought for her and the remarks about his purchase of a painting. She is so grateful that Richard hasn't pressed her, asking questions about that painting. Starting a cascade of lies is not what she wants to do. It isn't her personality or her character.

Richard and Gabby have sex that night. It is quick and lacks any romantic passion. It feels to her that Richard is claiming her as his own. The incident with Brett has sparked some green jealousy in Richard. Does Richard need to prove his love for her or does he want reassurance that their relationship is secure? Whatever the reason, she is more confused about their relationship than she has ever been. Afterward, while Richard lies sleeping, her mind drifts off, thinking of Brett. He is driving her crazy, and she wants answers to her questions. She cannot go on like this.

⟡⟡⟡⟡⟡⟡⟡

Back at his apartment, Brett pours another whiskey, sitting in his living room while staring at his newly acquired painting. He sits on his couch with his feet propped up, swirling his whiskey around and around in his glass. The Trinity Knot painting found a home above his fireplace. The canvas is the sole brightly colored item in the stark black-and-white modern décor. His thoughts go to Gabby as she permeates every part of his world. He can't escape her, even here in his condo, but that is his choice. He wants her in his world.

Earlier tonight, it took all of his effort to avoid getting into a verbal argument with Richard, if not a physical fight. He was stoked, as the feeling of power and the need for control could have easily overtaken him. He had gotten into some pretty bad brawls in the past due to his lack of self-control. Tonight, he controlled his actions. Why would he do anything to upset Gabby when he has tried so hard over the past few months to get in her good graces?

He smiles as he remembers her smile, her walk, and her scent. He loves the way she quivers from his touch. There is chemistry between them that cannot be denied. *How can I get her to admit that?* He looks once again at the painting. It has cost him three months' rent. *Well worth it*, he thinks while smiling and taking another sip of his whiskey. "It certainly brightens up the old place," he says aloud, and then adds, "Just like how my future with Gabby is going to brighten my life."

The following morning, Gabby goes to Art Smart. Rita greets her with a mug of coffee. "Good morning, Miss Gabby. Thanks to you, the gallery will stay open for another couple of months," she chimes as she hands Gabby the mug. Gabby knows she made a few sales but is not aware of the total. Rita gives Gabby a list of sales from the previous evening. Glancing at it, Gabby is aware of most of the sales except a few, and one of those is a very important one, her large Trinity Knot! There is no name listed behind the title, just SOLD, in bright red letters.

"Rita," she questions, "who bought my favorite Trinity Knot?"

"The buyer gave me cash for the purchase. I asked him for his information so I could put his name into our database, but the man declined. It did seem a bit odd, but maybe the painting is a surprise gift." Then Rita adds, "You know how folks make everyone's business their own in this town. Since it was for sale, I didn't think you would mind. Cash is always good."

"I just like to keep tabs on my paintings," Gabby says. Sad that her favorite painting isn't there, she feels like an orphan once again. That painting reminds her so much of her mother that it hurts knowing it is gone. Her eyes fill with tears, but she is determined not to let Rita see. Rita acting so casual about the transaction is upsetting. However, it isn't Rita's fault that the painting sold; it is Gabby's fault for hanging the painting and making it a part of the exhibition. It was her decision and her decision alone.

CHAPTER 8

It is a gorgeous, warm Sunday in January. That afternoon, the country club is having a huge fund-raiser for the local hospital. There will be hamburgers and hotdogs on the grill while a band plays country music. In addition, there is a raffle and a silent auction. Gabby gratefully offers a painting for the cause. She acquired her quest for philanthropy from her mother. Ever since she was old enough to remember, her mother supported local charities. Gabby loves this characteristic and wants to honor her mother's memory by always following suit.

The fund-raiser's featured event is a tennis match between the four male tennis pros. The four men will start by playing doubles for a set, then the winning team of that match will play against each other in a set of singles; the man standing as the sole winner will get the trophy along with the bragging rights. It will be a good time for both the pros and the spectators in addition to raising money for the hospital.

The center stadium court stands are filled, as it is a sold-out event. Gabby, Ella, and the rest of their team bought a block of tickets sitting together for the competitive match. As the tennis professionals are introduced, each one will saunter out in an outrageous-looking costume, and each will hold a bucket, collecting donations to benefit the children's ward at the hospital. It is customary for the pros to work the crowd, enticing them to donate more money for the cause. This usually involves giving hugs and kisses to the women and high-fives to the men. The pro who collects the most money will be rewarded a day off with pay. It is certainly beneficial to both the hospital and to the pro.

As they sit in the stands, Gabby's team of eight is there to totally support their drill coach. They are already discussing what they are going to do to Brett to have him earn their money. They are laughing and jokingly rehearsing how they will touch him and how long the kiss will be. Susie, one of the married players on the team, divulges information about the affair she had with Brett back in the fall. The rest of the team are curious and cock their ears to hear every word.

Meanwhile, Gabby looks away. It irritates her to listen as Susie discloses some of the more intimate details. When Susie finishes sharing, Ella turns to Gabby. Realizing that Gabby is lost in her own thoughts, Ella taps her on the shoulder, asking, "What are you going to do to Brett?"

"Truthfully," Gabby answers nonchalantly, "I really haven't thought much about it."

"Seriously, Gabby, you're telling me you haven't even considered it? I know you aren't a nun, so you must be crazy!" Ella belts with a shocked expression. "Oh, I get it now," she continues. "You are in love with Richard." Then she adds, "Well, unlike you, my dear friend, I am still looking for the love of my life. I have thought of nothing else but Brett. First, I think I'll start by grabbing him around the neck, then pulling his face toward mine and not letting go. I am going to get my full twenty dollars' worth. I have waited a long time to get this kiss. He is so hot, and at times, he acts as though he doesn't even know I'm alive. He will remember me after this. I guarantee it. This might be the start of something big."

"You and several hundred others," Gabby quips. Disappointed by Gabby's remark, Ella turns her attention to the activity on the court, joining in on the raillery with the other team members.

The anticipated fund-raiser has finally started. One after another, the pros come out on the court. Their outfits are both colorful and humorous: one has a Superman cape and mismatched socks. Another impersonates Andre Agassi and enters wearing all black and a long wig with headband. A third pro comes out dressed in drag with a long blond wig and a white skirt with green fishnet hose. And then it is Brett's turn. He saunters out wearing a hideous outfit—a blue-and-red, wide-striped shirt with yellow flowered shorts and bright pink knee-high socks. His hair is streaked with bright pink dye. Even though he is dressed in silly attire, his tan and muscles are clearly visible. The crowd is cheering, clapping, and laughing nonstop.

After a short announcement giving information about the charity and the events for the afternoon, the pros start to walk through the crowd collecting money. Their buckets are filling with cash. One member brings one hundred dollars in pennies, weighing down the bucket so much that the pro is having trouble. Finally, it is Brett's turn to approach the crowd. Slowly, he makes his way through the bleachers filled with admirers and tennis fans. The women and young girls are pulling and tugging on him. His eyes twinkle and he beams. His dimple seems even deeper as his wide smile is contagious. One after another, a girl hugs him, kisses him, and poses for a photo before giving him her precious bill. It is obvious that he enjoys being the center of attention.

In due time, he makes his way to Gabby and her teammates. As predicted, Ella jumps up first, grabbing him and then laying a kiss on him that seems endless. The crowd is encouraging, and the cheering and clapping are almost deafening. Ella emerges from the kiss glowing and makes him kiss her again, holding another bill above her head while a teammate shoots a photo. One by one, Brett makes his way along the row toward Gabby. Even Susie willingly offers her cheek to him while pinching him on his backside.

Now, as he stands facing Gabby, she has no way to avoid him. Timidly, she adds her money to the bucket; however, Brett waits. He keeps standing there in front of her. *Move on. Please, move on,* she thinks. *Move on to one of your groupies.*

He turns to face her. Lifting his eyebrows, he remarks, "It's your turn, Gabby. You know you want to," he says, offering his lips. She is unsuccessful in backing up as her legs are already pressed against the bleacher. He moves in closer and whispers, "How much of me are you buying?" His smirk stings, and her heart quickens as she remembers his past aggressive behavior. Her stomach churns. This time, she is able to push him away.

Out of the corner of her eye, she sees Ella staring, her arms crossed. Has Ella heard their hushed exchange? Gabby sighs in relief as Brett moves on down the row taking donations from spectators.

Ella asks with an inquisitive tone, sticking out her jaw, "What was that all about?"

"Nothing," Gabby says. "It was nothing." But it was something. The incident has unnerved her once again. Glancing at Brett, she sees that he looks back in her direction, smiling. Grateful that her teammates do not notice, she is relieved that they are busy texting and e-mailing, sharing their photos with friends and posting to the web.

After the donations are collected, it is time for the main event, the tennis matches. Brett and his partner win the doubles match. However, after a long fight, Brett loses the singles match in a tie-break. Gabby and the rest of her team enjoy watching Brett scramble on the court and cheer loudly when he makes a great shot. The fund-raiser is a huge success and after everything is totaled, the pros' collection buckets, the raffle, and the silent auction, the club has raised more than twenty thousand dollars for improvements to the hospital.

CHAPTER 9

A few weeks after the gallery reception, Brett goes back to the gallery in hopes of finding Gabby. Much to his dismay, she isn't there; however, Rita greets him with a huge motherly hug.

"How you doing there, Mr. Matthews?" she inquires. "Enjoying your new painting?" He looks her straight in the eye with a huge smile on his face; he cannot hide the pride he feels.

Rita continues, "You know, you really need to tell her. She's going to find out. I feel bad lying to her. You should have seen the disappointment on Gabby's face when I said I didn't know who bought her painting. Her heart dropped, and it took all I had not to give up the secret. She almost cried, and if that dear child had shed one tear, I would have told. That girl is like a daughter to me. If you hurt her, you'll be dealing with me. I have good feelings about you, so don't make me change my mind. You need to tell her."

Brett hugs Rita again, reassuring her that he will tell Gabby, and it will be soon. He just needs the timing to be right.

In the meantime, while they are talking, Gabby arrives at the gallery to start her shift. Shocked to find Brett there once again, she stands in silence.

"Hello, Gabby," Brett chimes in. "I was looking for you. If you have the time, I would love to buy you a cup of coffee. What do you say?"

Rita stands beaming, and as she nudges Gabby's arm, she states, "We're not busy at all. You two go ahead."

Brett reaches for Gabby while addressing Rita. "Thanks, I promise I won't keep her all afternoon."

The coffee shop is only a few doors away from the art gallery. Brett opens the door for Gabby and ushers her to the counter. The rich scent of freshly ground coffee fills the air. They order their drinks and wait in silence, not even looking at each other. Nervously glancing around at the tables, Gabby is relieved that there isn't anyone she recognizes. She can barely believe that she is here with Brett and cannot fathom his reason for searching her out. He motions her to find a table while he waits at the counter for their lattes.

Returning with the coffee, he is the first to speak. "Thanks for agreeing to meet with me."

"It's not like I had much of a choice," Gabby states firmly. "I wasn't going to cause a scene at the gallery in front of Rita." She stirs the froth on her coffee and avoids looking at him. She reaches into her purse, retrieving the box that holds the trinity knot earrings. Pushing the box toward Brett, she says, "Here, these belong to you. I cannot accept them."

"Keep them. I want you to have them," he replies as he pushes the box back over to her side of the table. "Really ... Gabby. I'm trying here. Can you meet me halfway?" he asks, searching for forgiveness once again. "I said I was sorry. Okay, I thought we were moving forward, and now it seems like we've taken a step backward. You don't even talk to me. It seems that you go out of your way to avoid me." Sadly, his green eyes are pleading his case more than the words he speaks. "Friends?" he asks, putting his hand out for her to shake.

Not extending her hand, she looks up, reading the lines of his face. She is in awe of his wide-set eyes and full lips. She sits staring at him, trying to collect the right words before blurting out something silly that she will later regret. Her heart is pounding, and her breaths are shallow. She has rehearsed this speech a million times since that day on the tennis court. She knew that this day was inevitable. Now she is finally face to face, having a conversation with her rapist. Carefully she speaks with all the courage she can muster. "Brett, you raped me and now you want to be friends? Explain to me, exactly how does that work ... we just pretend it never happened, is that it?"

He shifts his weight in his chair, puts his coffee cup down, and looks down into the murky brown liquid as if it is too much for him to look at Gabby. He opens his mouth, but the words seemingly refuse to depart his mouth.

He hangs his head in shame, stating, "I'm sorry. I'm so sorry."

She can feel his pain, and she can sense his anguish. His usual arrogant, confident self is nowhere to be found. She has trouble recognizing the face before her. Where is that effervescent charm? Even his dimple seems to have disappeared into the deep crease of shame masking his face. She searches her soul, trying to find a reason not to forgive, but her big compassionate heart refuses to remain hardened. Unconsciously, she reaches out her hand and finds his, giving it a squeeze. His hand is warm and strong. Her touch forces him to glance upward, and their eyes meet.

Minutes pass as they sit in silence with her hand still holding his, even though his eyes are focused on his coffee, avoiding her gaze. Finally, after uttering a word of thanks, Brett excuses himself. He pushes back his chair, stands, and slowly walks out the door, leaving her at the table alone.

Gabby is astonished as well as a bit perplexed, thinking back to her rage and shame from the rape and the days that followed—how she isolated herself, how her self-esteem plummeted, all of her anger and tears. Watching Brett agonizing and wallowing in some sort of self-defeat, her heart empathizes with his struggle. She thinks she is crazy to forgive but how can she not? Unless she is the world's worst judge of character, Brett comes across to her as being sincere and almost broken. Something terrible must have happened to cause him so much anguish and deep emotional pain. She opens the small box revealing the earrings. What a knotted mess. She places the box back in her purse.

Suddenly, thoughts of Richard pop into her mind. *Is Richard behind all of this?* Did he see the quick kiss between her and Brett? Richard has unlimited resources that he is known to use. His job as an attorney gives him easy access to detectives and public officials who can help him obtain police records and bank accounts. Has Richard looked into Brett's past and found something that he is using as leverage against him? Is this why Brett needed to speak with her? *Maybe, just maybe...*

Gabby, deep in thought, does not hear the door to the coffee shop open. Even the clatter of small bells hanging on the door does not break her trance. Seconds later, Ella, still in her tennis dress from her morning match, stares down at Gabby, snapping her fingers in Gabby's face. "Hey, you, I just ran into Brett in the parking lot," Ella says. She then looks down at the table and notices there are two cups of coffee in front of Gabby. "He was here with you. Now, I get it, you and Brett. No wonder you're acting so strange. You bitch. How can you do that to Richard? How can you do that to me?"

"Really, Ella, get a grip," Gabby scolds. "That's how rumors get started. Brett was at the art gallery and asked me to have coffee with him. That's all—nothing more."

"How do you always get so lucky," gasps Ella. "You know I want to have coffee with Brett and other things." She pauses. "I hear he is well-equipped in that department," she continues, giggling. "By the way, can I ask what you two talked about? You were so lost in thought you didn't even see me standing here."

"Well, if you would have come a few minutes sooner, I would have invited you to sit with us," Gabby casually replies, smiling, ignoring Ella's question. She is determined to downplay the incident as much as possible. The last thing she needs is a friend spreading rumors.

Not pressing her for an answer, Ella scoots into the booth across from her. "Gabby, I shouldn't tell you this and promise you won't tell Richard, okay? I just can't keep it to myself. Are you ready for this?"

Excited, she continues, "Richard talked to me the other day. He was asking me all kinds of questions about you: if I think you love him and if you are ready to settle down. I think he's getting ready to pop the big question. Isn't that exciting?" Ella almost screams the last part of her speech.

Gabby looks around the coffee shop to see if any of the customers have overheard before turning back to face Ella. "Really, he is asking you those kinds of questions? What did you tell him?"

Ella smiles. "I told him you are crazy about him." Without even stopping to take a breath or wait for a reaction, Ella proceeds. "What time of year do you think your wedding will be? I look best in dark colors so a winter wedding is good. Well, I guess you can have dark colors in the fall. A fall wedding doesn't give us much time to plan. Venues need to be booked at least a year in advance."

Ella and Gabby have discussed their wedding plans on numerous occasions back when they were at the university. It frequently became the subject after too much alcohol was consumed on a weekend night in their dorm. They would even buy bridal magazines and pretend to pick out dresses and flowers, vowing to be each other's maid of honor.

"Hey, slow down. He hasn't asked me yet, and I'm not sure I will say yes, even if he does. We have been arguing a lot lately," explains Gabby to her best friend.

"Everyone has arguments. That's why make-up sex is the best," adds Ella. "Of course you will marry him. Any girl would be happy to have Richard as a husband. Girl, I really don't understand you at times."

Quickly, Gabby realizes that trying to make Ella understand would be like trying to explain the game of chess to a toddler. Ella will never get it; for her, if a man is handsome and makes money, he is perfect. Thinking back through their history as friends, Gabby cannot recall a time when Ella was truly in love. Ella would profess to be in love one minute and then suddenly be out of love the next. In the past, Gabby has had difficulty keeping track of Ella's love interests; however, there is one thing that she is certain of—she knows that Ella wants Brett.

Quickly, she pushes back her chair, reaches over, and gives Ella a hug. "I've got to get back to the gallery," she says, excusing herself. "See you around," she calls over her shoulder.

"Later," Ella yells.

Before the gallery door can close as Gabby enters, Rita shouts, "Hey, you're back. How'd it go?" Rita searches for a smile on Gabby's face but finds none.

"We just talked," Gabby says, scanning the appointment book for meetings for the rest of the afternoon.

"Talked about what, your painting?" Rita continues happily.

"Honestly, Rita. No, we did not talk about painting or art or tennis. It seems like he wants to tell me something. Clearly, something is bothering him. I wonder if Richard is involved in any way," Gabby ponders, thinking aloud.

"Why on earth would you think that Richard might be involved with Brett?" questions Rita.

"After my reception, Brett was here with me. Richard walked through the door, and the two of them had a standoff. Richard was jealous and said some nasty things to Brett."

"What happened then?" Rita asks.

"Brett lied about buying a painting and excused himself like a gentleman."

"Really," remarks Rita. "He lied about buying a painting?"

Dusk is just falling, welcoming the arrival of another beautiful hill country evening. The restaurant on the lake is crowded, and live music will soon fill the air. It is his day off, and Brett wants to relax. At first, he listened attentively but now he fights back a yawn. Ella catches his smile; however, she's not aware of its sarcastic origin. She beams while continuing her torturous chatter. He exhales, his eyes shifting past her left shoulder as he gazes out at the water, hoping to find something more interesting, perhaps a boat docking or a group of young gals in bikinis. Anything to keep his mind occupied so he doesn't nod off. What was he thinking when he consented to this date? The annoying chatter continues.

He takes another swig of beer. Making Gabby jealous does not seem to be working. She goes out of her way to avoid him. He wanted to confess everything to her at the coffee shop, but how can he make her understand something that he really doesn't understand himself? He admits that things have gotten out of hand. He was so overpowered by his emotion and desire; he was just reacting. And as wrong as it may seem in hindsight, he followed through on those feelings with an aggressive sexual act. Gabby called it rape. Was it?

This incident has caused him to search his soul, find his need for power and control. He really wants to share his damaged past, but his pride will not allow this to happen. He has never told his story.

Ella has been very vocal about wanting a relationship with him. She has been flirting with him and touching him at every opportunity. Sure, she is easy on the eyes and feisty, but he isn't sure what else she brings to the table. She doesn't come from a wealthy family, so getting perks from dating her isn't going to happen. She is the girl you screw when you are horny, not the one you take home to meet your family. But isn't that what he enjoys? No commitments, just sex? No, not since he met Gabby. Why is Gabby making him act differently?

Ella taps her glass with her nails. "Well?" she asks again.

Brett's attention returns. "Sorry, I didn't hear you."

When she tries to repeat her question, he interrupts. "Let's get out of here."

"I want to stay and hear the band. Please, let's stay," Ella begs. "I went to school with two of the musicians." He ignores her protests, pushes his chair back, and heads for the exit, letting her follow if she wants to come along.

Leaving the lights off upon entering his apartment, Brett pulls her in for a kiss while his hand reaches up under her short skirt, caressing her upper thigh and buttocks. She giggles and helps him by pulling her blouse over her head. However, when bringing her arms down, Ella's arm hits something hard. She screams, "Ouch!" and there is a huge crash. Brett quickly finds the light switch. He curses when he finds his bike sprawled on the floor.

"I'm so sorry," Ella says as she and Brett collide, trying to upright the bike. While he is inspecting it to be sure all the parts are intact, Ella, curious about his bachelor's pad, glances up and gasps, "You have one of Gabby's paintings." Then she asks, "When did she give it to you?"

The chatter has started again. *Gabby, Gabby, Gabby.* He has tried so hard to get that girl out of his mind. All of his attempts to get with her have failed. Ella was to be the perfect distraction, but this is not working. He curses the bike for ruining his pursuit and also for Ella giving Gabby center stage once again.

He continues his chase, reaching for Ella's breast. Her black lacy bra is trying to push his thoughts of Gabby out of his mind, but his pride forces him to answer. "No, she didn't give it to me." Trying again, he leans in, pressing against her, seeking her lips to stop the chatter.

Ella is surprised. "You bought it?"

He abruptly stops, backs up, and looks at her, answering, "Yes, I bought it."

"You're kidding, right?" Ella continues, trying to understand. Brett turns away. "Where are you going?" she demands.

"To get a drink. I lost my focus," he answers as he walks out of the room.

Ella, standing alone, stares at the painting, shaking her head as she buttons her blouse.

CHAPTER 10

Richard and Gabby returned their RSVP for the Valentine's Ball at the country club weeks ago. It is a grand affair, the most impressive party of the year. Richard balks at going, and she isn't sure why but is pleased that he finally consented to go. As an attorney, his job gives him opportunities with invitations to many social affairs where he is polite and engaging, but he is often bored, and if given his preference, he would rather be home. Gaining new clients and networking are his only motivations for attending parties.

Another reason Richard isn't fond of attending galas is that dancing is usually involved. To ease this chasm, Gabby suggested they take couples dancing lessons so they can enjoy the activity she loves. She loves the movement the music invokes within her. She loves the freedom fast-dancing allows her while duly enjoying the closeness and intimacy of slow-dancing. "Even two perfect strangers touch on the dance floor," she whispered into Richard's ear after much coaxing, finally getting him swaying on the dance floor with her.

Gabby, a true romantic, enjoys the festive atmosphere of the ballroom. Approaching the entrance, she hears the orchestra playing in the background with the entire room carefully set to the holiday theme. She enjoys the scent of the flowers, as arrangements are everywhere, standing tall, welcoming all who enter.

This year, the club has snubbed the traditional red and opted for pink roses that stand proudly in tall square glass containers on each table. Accompanying the roses are crystals of clear glass, hanging as if kissing the roses with their reflective light. Silver sprigs are scattered throughout the bouquets, giving the richness that only precious metal can convey, adding just the right amount of bling so as not to overtake the delicacy of the roses. Pink roses are Gabby's favorite, and her mind delights in being surrounded with their presence. The many mirrors on the ceiling enhance the beauty of it all.

How wonderful this all seems, almost surreal. It is the grand ballroom, and grand it is indeed. The club has certainly gone to great lengths to show off its premiere event, as the Valentine's Ball is the most attended event of the entire year, bigger even than the elaborate holiday parties. The women arrive wearing beautiful, draping gowns, and the men dapper in their tuxedos. It surely is a majestic sight. The club even opted for men in black tails and white gloves to assist the members arriving in taxis and limos.

Gabby is glad that she is one of the first to arrive, so she can soak it all in before the crowds of partygoers will obscure the beauty of the room. She has taken a taxi to the club alone as Richard gave her an ever-familiar text message: "Go on without me, working. I will meet you later." When seeing this on her phone, she rolled her eyes. *Really, Richard, just tell the truth. You really don't want to be here, so you will dash in late and leave early.* That is Richard's ammo, and if he thinks he's fooling her with this familiar routine, he is wrong. Gabby isn't going to let Richard's pessimistic attitude toward the ball bring her down. She looks forward to this event every year, and nothing is going to steal her joy.

She smiles back at the men who nod approvingly as she passes by. Her strapless ivory gown clings to her perfect figure. Its sweetheart bodice is made of chiffon, fitted at the waist, and then yards of ivory satin flow to the floor. Her tanned olive skin sparkles as tiny golden flecks shimmer on her upper chest and shoulders. She wears her gold trinity knot necklace as always, with simple diamond studs in her ears, and a single strand tennis bracelet adorns her wrist.

While dressing, she tried to wear the diamond pendant necklace that Richard had given her the evening after he missed their anniversary celebration, but she couldn't overcome her feelings of betrayal. After clasping it around her neck and turning to gaze in the mirror, all she could see was the showy, expensive piece. It looked out of place. It was an impostor. She wanted something more genuine. Quickly, she removed the pendant, placed it back in its original box, and reached for her familiar trinity knot necklace.

With her jewelry selection made, she completed her outfit with a pair of golden Stewart Weitzman sandals with a four-inch spiked heel. She could easily be mistaken for a Neiman's model, as she is simply stunning. She chose to wear her long blond hair up in a twist with loose curls dangling. Adding a spray of her favorite Chanel was the last step. She is a knockout. She is clueless of the effect she has on members of the opposite sex. Her looks, combined with her outgoing personality and kind heart, makes her the full package.

Gabby works the room, talking at length to friends. She gets slightly annoyed by the questions others ask inquiring about Richard's whereabouts. "He has to work late, and he will be here soon," is always her standard response while smiling. This usually satisfies even the most inquisitive folks.

Getting away from the big band era, the orchestra is beginning to play tunes that are more modern. Gabby looks at the dancing couples, watching as she hopes to see the glimmer in their eyes as they dance with one another. She has read that couples who are really in love cannot help but stare into their loved ones' eyes, searching to find themselves deep within.

Caught in her daydream, she nearly chokes on her wine when she sees Brett dancing with a beautiful, tall blonde. Gabby doesn't recognize her, but as a pro at the club, Brett is required to attend the ball and dance with the ladies to help drum up business. What better place to get a lady to commit to a few lessons as he is dazzling her with his good looks, including that dimple, and of course, his charm. It is only a bonus that he is also a credible dancer. He can get even the least coordinated woman looking and feeling like she is Cinderella. How would Gabby feel if Brett were sweeping her across the floor? She steals another look at him and the blonde.

She admits he does look fabulous. His tux is black with an edging of darker black trim along the lapels, with a white ruffled shirt. He wears a bolo tie instead of the traditional bow tie, giving in to that cowboy charm that he likes to display. Completing his outfit is a pair of black cowboy boots with just a bit of heel to them, making him appear taller and even more desirable to members of the opposite sex. In his right ear, he wears a diamond earring. He shines as brightly as the full moon on a clear summer's eve. Watching him effortlessly sweep his partners around the floor makes Gabby think of Richard. *I wish he were a better dancer.* Reminded once again of Richard, she scans the ballroom trying to spot him. Her eyes travel from the room back to the front double door. *Two hours late.* She frowns.

Distracting her from her thoughts, Ella starts pulling on Gabby's elbow. "Well, don't you look absolutely gorgeous," Ella stammers, stepping back to get a full panoramic view.

"You look pretty awesome yourself, Ella," exclaims Gabby, giving her best friend a warm hug. Ella is dressed in a beautiful turquoise pleated gown that falls in a drape off her creamy white shoulders. The color is a perfect accent to her thick, short brunette waves.

Ella continues excitedly, "I get to dance with Brett next! I wish he would stop ogling that blonde he's dancing with now. I swear if her cleavage is any more prominent, we will be taking the old guys out of here on stretchers." After making this statement, Ella readjusts her dress exposing more of her bosom. "We had a date last week."

"Really?" Gabby replies, intrigued. "How did that go?" she asks, taking another sip of her wine.

"Not at all the way I thought it would go. I barely got to first base," Ella says, glancing at Brett dancing with the blonde. Looking back at Gabby, she continues, "He was a bit moody. I thought we were there to hear the band, but he got up and left before the music started." Ella sees Gabby also looking out on to the dance floor.

"Did you dance with him yet?" Ella inquires.

Gabby answers as if in deep thought. "Nope. Don't think I am going to," she adds, not looking back at Ella.

Ella smiles but continues as she tries to understand. "I didn't know he was such a Gabby fan."

"What do you mean by that?" Gabby asks with a raised brow, looking back at her friend. Ella has certainly gotten her attention.

"His interest in your painting," Ella continues.

"That's right, he was at my reception, but then lots of people were there."

Ella changes the subject. "Hey, where's Richard?"

"Late as usual," Gabby says, forcing a smile, trying to act unconcerned as she takes another sip of her wine. Then she adds, "Working. Who really knows?"

After making excuses for Richard's absence, she reassures Ella. "Ella, you look gorgeous. Brett will only have eyes for you." This seems to calm her friend down a bit until Ella spies Brett coming toward them.

"Here I go," Ella says. "Wish me luck."

Gabby notices how Ella seems to float across the gap into Brett's arms. She has to admit what she is feeling is jealousy as she watches her best friend's face beaming. Ella lifts her eyes to meet Brett's. Gabby forces a smile, and Ella looks over Brett's shoulder, winking back at her.

CHAPTER 11

Richard will be late for the Valentine's Ball, but he always intended to be late. Tuxedos and dancing are not high on his list. He would rather finish a brief at the office. His choice to work late requires his administrative assistant to stay late, as there is some editing to do before sending the papers by express mail for an early morning arrival to the client.

Carol, a single woman, is a few years younger than Gabby. Carol enjoys working at the law office and teases and flirts with the lawyers who are still bachelors. She has tried to get Richard's attention on many occasions: writing notes, brushing up against him, offering compliments and requests to go out for drinks at the end of their workday. Richard would be a liar if he said this does not attract him.

Today, Carol dressed for work in a short black leather skirt with a zipper running in a diagonal up the front, getting every hot-blooded guy wondering if that zipper really works. Could they unzip it and open that skirt to show her long, thin legs encased in thigh-high nylon stockings that she likes to show off whenever she bends over to grab a file in the bottom of the cabinet? Richard gets aroused just thinking about it, and he has thought about it several times that day. His state of arousal is almost continuous and reminds him of his lack of sex with Gabby over the past few weeks. He needs sex soon or he will go crazy.

Carol enters his office and ever so gently closes the door behind her. Richard, distracted with his work, does not notice at first but becomes aware of the strong scent of her perfume. It reminds him of a field of flowers, and he does enjoy both women and the smell of flowers. She walks around behind the desk to massage his back.

"You poor baby," she coos. "You work so hard. It must be so tough on you. Let me loosen these muscles a bit."

He is not surprised, as she has done this several times before. Her touch makes his arousal that much more intense. Turning around to get her to stop, his face is even with her breasts. She has on a white blouse, and she has seductively unbuttoned the top three buttons. He feasts his eyes on her cleavage and the lace trim of her bra.

She takes this opportunity to position herself between Richard and his desk, sliding his computer to the far end as she seats herself facing him. He can look up that skirt and see the lace tops of her hose. Instantly, he places his hands on her legs and slowly moves them up to the top of her nylons. Carol encourages him by pushing on his back, pressing him closer. She groans in a deep throaty voice, and he pulls on the end of that zipper on her skirt with his mouth.

To his amazement, the zipper does work. He can feel each tooth of the zipper open as he tugs on the flap. After opening her skirt to her panties, Carol reaches for him and kisses him, and kisses him deeply, as she takes his hands and pushes them up higher on her thighs, right to her lace thong. He winds the lace around his finger, pulling the panties to the side, releasing her secret parts for him to caress. Eagerly, she parts her legs, and he steps closer to her. She quickly unbuckles his belt and pulls down his zipper.

He enjoys her tongue as it playfully dances, and he pushes himself farther into her warm cavity. His hand on her silky brown hair, he pushes her head, matching his rhythm. Close to culmination, he stops her. Pulling her upright and staring into her eyes for an instant, he whispers something about being careful. He is thinking of using a condom, but he is too far gone to stop now. Likewise, Carol places her finger over his lips, hushing Richard as he tries to voice his concerns. However, he is fast approaching his sexual fulfillment.

Suddenly, he rolls her over onto her stomach and approaches her from behind. One hand grabs her breast, and he uses his other to position himself at just the right angle, pushing himself into her, thrusting deep and hard. Within seconds, he has his release, filling her. Not wishing to discuss his actions, he hurriedly walks away, leaving Carol leaning over his desk, trying to regain her composure.

CHAPTER 12

Gabby is startled when someone comes up behind her and touches her ever so lightly on the shoulder. Turning around to face her father, she sees the concern on his face, knowing he has sensed her unhappiness. King asks lovingly in his low Texan drawl, "What's wrong, kitten?"

He's called her that ever since she was a little girl. Wayne King is a tall man, standing six-foot-two with broad shoulders. He is still considered handsome even though his long hours out in the sun have wrinkled his skin, giving him the same look as one of Gabby's favorite worn purses. He didn't remarry after Gabby's mother died, but he does occasionally have a lady friend—his words—that he takes to the movies or to dinner.

Continuing with his questions, King inquires, "Where is your attorney?"

Gabby's face shows no hint of a smile, and the horizontal shaking of her head accompanied by an eye roll speaks more than words. Her father puts his arm behind the small of her back and whisks her out onto the dance floor.

"Kitten, you are the most beautiful woman in the room," her father whispers quietly into her ear.

Turning to face him, she finally smiles and says, "You always say that."

"That's because it's true," he coos and chuckles as he twirls her around playfully.

"Feelin' better?" he asks after giving her another twirl.

"Yes, you know I love to dance."

"That I do know. You got that from your old man." He winks.

Halfway through the dance with her father, Richard arrives and taps King on the shoulder. "May I cut in?" he asks in a mild manner. Gabby's father reluctantly hands her over to Richard and bows as he leaves, searching for his daughter's approval.

◇◈◇◈◇◈◇◈◇

After leaving the dance floor, King heads to the bar, taking a seat beside Brett.

"Young man, is it my imagination or are you staring at me ... or my daughter? I'll presume it's the latter. Lovely creature, isn't she? Can't seem to understand why she stays with that schmuck," King states, pointing to Richard. "I'm having whiskey," King says, motioning to the bartender. "Pour one for my friend here, too. How do you know Gabby?" he asks Brett.

Shyly, Brett answers, "The tennis club where I—"

King cuts in before Brett has a chance to go on. "Oh, yes, now I remember. You're the tennis pro Gabby was telling me about."

Brett buries his face in his whiskey glass.

King inquires, "You really a cowboy or do you just dress like one?"

"Real cowboy, sir. Well, I used to be. I grew up on a ranch just west of here. Learned to ride and rope before I could walk."

"You ride anymore?" asks King.

"Not for a while," Brett says. "I haven't been to a ranch since I left for college more than a decade ago."

"Shame," King adds. "Man finds himself out riding the range, gives him time to think and get some direction in his life. You married?"

"No, sir," Brett quickly responds.

"Good. You free tomorrow?" King doesn't wait for him to reply. "Come on out to the ranch. You can show me if you're worthy of those boots you are wearing."

"Working in the morning, sir," Brett says. "But the afternoon—"

King cuts in again, handing Brett a business card. "Great, see you there. Here's my card. Call my secretary to get directions. Plan on spending the night. We're gonna have a hoedown—barbecue, music, beer, and fireworks. Gabby loves Valentine's Day. It's her favorite holiday, so I like to make it special for her."

"But, sir ..." stammers Brett.

King, using his cowboy hat, slaps Brett on the thigh and says, "Bring some riding clothes, cowboy. It's like riding a bicycle, you never forget."

Brett does miss those days on the ranch. He could ride as well as any. He could rope a cow and tie it in record time. He would spend entire days on Diesel, a tall chestnut-brown stallion, riding the perimeter of the ranch, helping the men by checking the fences for holes and rescuing any cattle that had escaped or had gotten their long horns tangled in the wild brush. He enjoyed riding the open country with the fresh air and the full sun.

⬦⬦⬦⬦⬦⬦⬦

"Where have you been?" Gabby asks Richard. "The ball is almost over."

"Working," he replies.

She continues in an annoyed voice but smiling all the while as they move slowly across the dance floor. "You know how important this night is to me. It's the best ball of the year."

Richard stops in his tracks and looks at her, pleading. "Let's not fight. Not here and not now." Immediately, he bends down on one knee, opens a small black velvet box, and asks, "Gabby, will you marry me?"

"Marry you? You ask me now after waltzing in here hours late, smelling of another woman's perfume?"

"I thought this is what you want. Well, isn't it?"

"What do you want, Richard? We haven't exactly been getting along lately. You have been so busy with your work and I have been—"

"You have been what, Gabby? Distant, uncaring. You've changed. If it's a ring you want—"

"A ring. You think this is all about a ring? It isn't. It's about the way you treat me and care for me, or rather the way you *don't* care for me. I can't do this anymore. I'm not okay with your cheating. I deserve far better. You aren't good enough for me, Richard."

"Well," he shouts loud enough for others to hear, "if you were more compassionate, maybe I wouldn't need to cheat!" Here it is again, Richard placing all of the blame on her for his indiscretions.

Getting up off his knee and realizing that they are causing a scene, he closes the black velvet box and walks away, leaving Gabby alone and speechless in the middle of the dance floor. She can feel the stares all around. She needs to get out of there fast.

She escapes through the double doors and finds herself alone on the patio. Leaning up against the wrought iron railing, she breathes a deep breath. Breaking it off with Richard felt wondrously good; instead of fighting back tears, her body heaves a sigh of relief. The night air is cool and refreshing. The music from the crowded ballroom wafts from the clubhouse and disguises Brett's footsteps as he draws near.

He stands behind her, whispering in her ear, "A penny for your thoughts."

Even though she cannot hear him approach, her other senses are on high alert. Her body feels his presence long before he speaks. She smells his spicy scent and feels her heart skip a beat. Breathing in deeply, she vows not to turn around, keeping her back to him. Standing exactly where she is, she needs to contemplate her next move in this unspoken game they have been playing over the past few months. She decides to hold her position, forcing him to make the next move. And he does, taking the lead, positioning himself another step closer. She feels the warmth of his body brushing her exposed back. He slides his arms close to her sides, reaching the railing, trapping her. Smiling, she curses herself for giving him the upper hand, as once again she has no escape.

"You okay?" he asks. She feels his breath on her neck and is intoxicated by him. "That was quite a scene in there."

"I'm better than I thought," she manages to say with a nervous quiver in her voice.

Taking his hands away from the railing, Brett places them on her hips, turning her around to face him. In a low voice, he makes a single request. "Dance with me, beautiful lady. I came to dry your tears but, alas, there are none. The night is still young, and the music is inviting. Dance with me."

Reaching for her right hand with his left, he twirls her around, his eyes gleaming, while humming along with the song, drawing her body closer toward his chest. Placing his chin on the top of her hair, he continues to waltz her gracefully around the porch. His humming turns into words as the band is playing Brian Adam's song, "When You Really Love a Woman." Brett sings along and she is surprised that his voice is quite good.

The dance they share is light and without effort. Gabby blames her light-headedness on a combination of the wine she consumed and the twirling movements. Maybe she is flying, and Brett is soaring right beside her.

Ironically, she feels safe in his arms, telling herself to let go and relax, enjoy this present moment under the star-filled sky. Knowing she must, she lifts her eyes to meet his. He stops singing and time stands still; neither one of them has to say a word. She finds his eyes, searching to see if she can see part of herself in them. His eyes dance with delight and unexpectedly, her body cleaves closer. She feels his manhood pressing hard against her thigh.

Their bodies don't stop swaying when the music ceases. Gabby is still emotionally vulnerable, but she vows to live in this moment. She will deal with the consequences tomorrow. Why does she have compassion for him? She understands that he is damaged. She felt this during their conversation at the coffee shop. Is she a fool to believe that he is a good person? Tonight, dancing and kissing Brett makes her feel alive.

Once more, he probes her mouth with his tongue dancing, losing himself in her warmth and beauty. He is so smitten he can barely stand, drunk on Gabby's embrace. Her arms reach around his neck, pulling him in closer.

He abruptly backs away, seemingly in anguish. Gabby is stunned.

"I've got to go," he stammers, leaving her staring at the closing door he just exited.

CHAPTER 13

After escaping, Brett quickly finds the men's room and locks the stall door behind him. He feels the familiar rush of power, and he must control it. The animal he unleashed on the porch with Gabby still stirs within. He bangs his head on the bathroom stall door, curses and prays, *Please let me be here alone,* not wanting any witnesses to his outburst. He stands with his back against the door, and then he does something he never did before—he cries. Tears stream down his face and he stifles his sobs, sucking in his breath.

Remembering his college tennis coach's words that behavior equals consequences gave him the self-discipline tonight to back away. He has hurt her once before and has vowed to change, never giving her cause to be hurt by him again.

He cries for the little innocent boy who suffers from within. He cries for the night he had no control and was raped by a fellow ranch hand, a man he trusted and whom his father trusted. He remembers the quickness of the sexual act, his embarrassment, and his guilt. He remembers it all as if it just happened yesterday. Brett never told anyone. His secret is buried from the world, but he cannot bury it from himself. It stays with him, always lurking in the darkest part of him.

Tonight, walking away was difficult. Gabby makes him want to be a better man. Does she understand how important she is to him? He has worked months to repair the damage he caused between them. In the time they spent together, he feels a yearning and desire that is worth more to him than a few seconds of power and control. He desires to have more of her, all of her. He wants to look at her, talk to her, touch her, and kiss her. He wants to care for her, protect her, and, yes, love her. He wants all of her, and he needs her to want him.

His motivation tonight for walking away was to show her that he can change and has changed. If he wants her to love him, he needs to give her time.

Gabby regains her composure, trying to settle her racing heart and her rapid breathing. She needs to get her feet back on the ground, wondering what went wrong that forced Brett to leave so abruptly. She is puzzled. Stroking her hair and smoothing her dress, she walks back to the ballroom. Everything in the room pales against what she experienced before. The ball no longer holds its appeal. She doesn't notice the gaiety of the guests, the fragrance of the pink roses, or the twinkly lights. She needs to be alone. Relieved to cross the room without a confrontation, she exits the club. She is thankful for the waiting cab, and she sighs in relief when it turns the corner into the dark night.

Arriving at their shared condo, she confirms Richard's absence. She is relieved, as she has braced herself for an argument. Now, she earnestly prays Richard will stay out all night. Dealing with him is not her first priority, as thoughts of Brett dance in her head, overshadowing all else. She smiles, reliving her moments with him: their dance, their kiss, and their shared sexual arousal. Her soul craves to remember every detail, giving each great consideration. She feels alive and happy.

Being with Brett excites her and scares her at the same time. Her mind is spinning. Her perfect college GPA validates her intelligence; however, remembering Richard's words about how she is encouraging Brett, she wonders if she is only asking for more trouble down the road. She struggles with starting a serious relationship with him. The rape is like a huge boulder blocking the road. The danger signs are everywhere, and many would consider her a fool for venturing down this path. Why is she drawn to him? If he had raped other women at the club, wouldn't she have gotten wind of the gossip? With the other women enjoying the attention he gives to them, Gabby doesn't think this possible. Who is this guy?

This newfound excitement makes her aware of the passion missing from her current relationship with Richard. Disappointed that she has wasted precious years in a relationship with him, she ponders exactly when their relationship died. How long have they been going through the motions, pretending they were close? These new stirrings of love and sexual desire confirm her unfulfilled appetite; she has been starving for love. Taking a deep breath, she inhales, catching Brett's lingering scent, denying her thoughts as mere fantasy.

It is real, but it is dangerous. Brett is a bad boy—one she vows never to engage in a relationship. Not forgetting that he has raped her, she must be crazy to even contemplate being alone with him. She should have sought out a counselor. Maybe she isn't strong enough or healthy enough to see the situation clearly. There is no denying the arousal she feels. How can something that feels so good be so wrong?

She reaches for a cool glass of water to help settle her thoughts, knowing that she needs to pack for the weekend at her family's ranch, which is only a two-hour drive from Austin. She loves the ranch: the endless fields, the blue sky, the grazing horses, and the cactus. Tomorrow at the ranch, she can escape from both Richard and Brett. She needs to think, and there is no better place to think but in open spaces.

Safely back in his condo, Brett kicks off his boots, unbuttons his shirt, and throws his tuxedo jacket over the back of his couch. He flops down, sinking into the couch, and pours himself a hefty portion of whiskey from the bottle on the coffee table, emptying his glass with one huge gulp. He feels the fire of the whiskey burning; however, it burns less intensely than the rage that burns within. For years, he tried to keep those inner coals to a smolder but tonight a spark of desire ignited, and the buried turmoil and confusion along with humiliation leaped up into a ferocious fire.

His past is something that he cannot escape. The memories of the molestation keep flooding his inner being, stirring unrest. He tells himself to just deal with it and get over it as he was just an innocent kid who was in the wrong place at the wrong time. But his continual, impulsive sexual behavior is evidence that his thinking is flawed. Even though his mind tells him the rape wasn't his fault, secretly, his emotions keep convicting him and branding him guilty.

Reaching for the whiskey once again, he looks at Gabby's painting above his fireplace. At this moment, he can relate to the golden fire that glows from within the Trinity Knot, making him smile. One day he will be sure to ask Gabby her interpretation. Rita mentioned this painting is Gabby's favorite, and Brett longs to understand. He has already seen her emotional attachment to the necklace, and he is certain both the necklace and the painting represent something almost sacred to her. He pours the remainder of the whiskey bottle into his glass as he throws his cuff links on the coffee table, hearing the metal click on the glass top. Again, his thoughts go to Gabby as he takes another sip. He wants her in his world.

Remembering the offer from Wayne King to visit the King Ranch tomorrow for the hoedown, Brett is reminded of his former life.

With these thoughts fresh in his mind, he walks to the hall closet and digs far in the back for a hidden cardboard box. He grabs his pocketknife, then cuts the tape, and the flaps spring open. He cannot remember the last time he viewed the contents of this box. It was many years before, when he left the ranch for college on his tennis scholarship.

Presently, he is thankful for the numbing effects of the whiskey dulling his emotions. His hope of spending precious time with Gabby tomorrow at the ranch is the only thing that pushes him to reach inside the box, retrieving one object at a time. He fills his coffee table with the trophies in various sizes and ribbons of different colors. He is surprised as he handles each one, feeling pride in the accomplishments they represent. Maybe time, along with the help of the whiskey, has taken the pain of that former life away from these physical reminders. Examining each object, Brett reminisces about his moments in the arena, accepting his awards for his outstanding skills and performance in riding and roping.

In the bottom of the box, he sees the photo. As a teen, he had that photo taped to his headboard, and he had looked at it every night, validating his success. It was the photo when he received his trophy from the Rodeo Princess. God, it's been years since he last had it in his hands. It is yellowed and crinkled. He smiles as he sees the sweet little girl in the photo handing him his trophy. *Does she remember?*

Thinking of the ranch and the life he left behind is bittersweet. He loved the open country and the horses. He smiles, remembering the pride in his father's face the day he won the trophy, but quickly his smile fades as his father's face is replaced with the face of the man Brett wishes to forget, turning his fond memories into mere ashes yet again. That man's face haunts Brett's waking thoughts and has haunted his sleep for over a decade. He can trace every wrinkle in the man's face and can smell the mixture of sweat, booze, and cigarettes. He can still feel the man's rough hands as they covered his mouth, muffling his cries for help. He can still feel the scratchy hay beneath his face as the ranch hand held him down and raped him. With a jolt,

Brett shakes his head to aid in shaking the image out of his mind. He is breathing hard, and a bead of sweat forms on his forehead.

Suddenly, he turns and lashes out, knocking the trophies off the coffee table. Quickly gathering them, he throws them along with the ribbons back into the box. Years ago, when as a teenager he originally put the trophies and ribbons out of sight, he vowed never to return to the ranch life. He wants to forget. But now, things in his life are changing. He is well aware that if he wants to see Gabby, he needs to face his fears and put the past behind him. He will need to be strong, breaking that vow he made more than a decade ago. He looks again at the photo and drops it on the table next to his cuff links.

Even though it is well past midnight, Brett lifts the box and heads to the dumpster. It was silly for him to hide these away. He should have disposed of them years ago. This part of his life has not only robbed him of his dream of performing in the rodeo circuit, but he has allowed this part of his life to still cause him pain. He is not going to let his past rob him of his dreams again. With great force, he hurls the box with its tainted treasures into the dumpster. Wiping his hands, he takes a deep breath and is astonished that he is feeling relief. He turns around, walks back to his apartment door, and doesn't look back.

With reservation, he plans to take Wayne King up on his offer to visit the ranch. He will just enjoy the present moment, keeping his desire to be near Gabby the focus of the day, pushing the bad memories far back in his mind. It will be a challenge, but one that he must accept. He is not going to give up. He is going to fight and this time, he will win that fight.

He awakes the next morning hung over. The sun is high in the sky. The clock lets him know that he forgot to set his alarm and will have to rush to teach his Saturday morning tennis drill. Quickly he dresses, forgoing his shower, and heads out the door without his usual morning coffee.

It is another beautiful Texas morning, and he knows it would be a perfect day to go out on the ranch. Putting the top down on his convertible, he thinks, *Only in Texas can February be this good!*

His lesson goes rather smoothly, for which he is grateful in his compromised state. Several of Gabby's teammates, including Ella, attend. Brett was hopeful that Gabby would also be present at the drill, but her name was not on the roster handed to him by the front desk personnel.

Today, Ella does not flirt with him in her usual manner but seems to pout. They have been very guarded around one another since their date a few weeks ago. After months of their verbal foreplay during lessons, that anticipated date turned out to be terribly disappointing. Now, they must rebuild their friendship. Since Ella is Gabby's best friend, if Brett is seriously thinking of a relationship with Gabby, he had better make amends with Ella. He smiles at her and tries to make light of the tension.

Teasingly, he comments on the prior evening's ball. "Someone's a little edgy today. Did you drink too much or just not get enough sleep?"

With scorn in her voice, she corrects him in a rather hostile manner, exclaiming, "It's not the booze, Brett. It's *you!*"

Taken aback, he asks, "Hey, what's going on?" She looks at him closed-mouthed and stomps away, leaving him bewildered. He can't recall an unpleasant incident with Ella last night. From their dance, he was led to believe the episode at his apartment had been resolved. He twirled her around the dance floor twice, and she seemed happy and didn't mention anything was wrong.

Shaking his head, he continues the lesson, ignoring her outburst. "Women," he mutters, shaking his head again, this time accompanying it with an eye roll.

PART 11
The Set

CHAPTER 14

Every spring, Wayne King throws an old-fashioned western hoedown, complete with a barbecue, a band, and a bonfire. All the nearby ranchers and their families are invited along with King's business partners and friends. It is a grand affair and one the locals look forward to every year. After the food and dancing, there will be fireworks, filling the sky with their colors and sparkle accompanied by their loud bang.

A weekend at the ranch is just what Gabby needs to give some clarity to her life. She will have time to think and put things in their proper perspective, and hopefully, have a long talk with her dad. He has always helped her gain some objectivity, and she needs his help now more than ever. Thinking of her father always makes her smile. With her breakup with Richard less than a day old and new feelings surfacing for Brett, she is emotionally exhausted and excited at the same time. "I really need to get away," she hears herself saying to the walls in her condo as she turns to the door with her suitcase in hand.

Turning her SUV from the main road through the opened double gate bearing the King brand, a crown with two horseshoes, she breathes a deep breath and after letting it out slowly, sighs as it feels good to be back home. The drive to the ranch from Austin with the windows down offered her a warm spring breeze, and already she feels much better. There is nothing better than home sweet home. The paved drive to the ranch house is a much-welcomed modern addition. In her youth, the drive was a single-lane country road that would fill the air with so much dust, one could barely see let alone breathe. She drives slowly, enjoying the land with the cedars and cactus, trying to get a glimpse of some longhorns. It is too early in the season for the plentiful bluebonnets, but signs of spring are visible as everything is starting to show new life after the cold winter.

Gabby pulls up in the circular drive in front of the ranch house. She takes a minute, pondering her life when she lived here as a girl. She remembers the ranch house well. The porch leads to large wooden double doors. Through these doors, guests are greeted by an open great room that is connected to a dining room big enough to seat a dozen comfortably. The only other rooms on the main floor are the kitchen and her father's small office. The kitchen is the busiest room in the house as there is always some delicious smell coming from food cooking on the stove or baking in the ovens. Every Friday evening, Gabby used to help her mother prepare a meal for the ranch hands as a gesture of thanks for their hard work.

Finally, on the left side of the great room, a single curved stairway leads the way to an open balcony on the top floor. Upstairs, there are four bedrooms, two on each side, and each with its own bathroom. From the time of her childhood, Gabby has had dreams of walking down this staircase with her father waiting at the bottom, offering his arm to escort her to a nervous groom on her wedding day. Even though the dream is ever present, it has faded a bit as life events unfolded for her over the past few years. At this age, she had always pictured herself married with kids, but now with her art career just starting to take off and with the break-up with Richard, it seems an even more distant dream.

In addition to the ranch house, a few hundred feet down the lane are the barn and the bunkhouse, which houses a dozen ranch hands. The ranch is about three hundred thousand acres and requires a lot of upkeep. Since Gabby's mother died, her father bought a townhouse in the city and commutes between the two residences. His faithful foreman, Rusty Jones, who has been with him for nearly two decades, lives in the main house along with his wife, Jamie. They keep the ranch in tip-top shape, and King is ever so grateful for their loyalty and for their willingness to live there. He believes in the wise old fable that says a good ranch needs people who love it, and in return, the ranch will return their love sevenfold.

Gabby races out of her parked car and up the porch steps, pushes through the front door of the house, and calls her father's name. No reply. She calls for Rusty or Jamie but still no reply. Lifting her bag, she jogs up the curved staircase to her room. The adjacent room is her dad's while the rooms on the opposite side of the house are occupied by Rusty and his wife.

Her room is kept as it was when she was growing up. She loves this room. She glances around, finding comfort in the familiar surroundings. White chair rails and ceiling moldings accent the sky-blue walls. White eyelet curtains with matching bedspread and pillows complete the décor. She places her suitcase gently on the navy carpet as she studies the wall of artwork, representing a diary of her life.

Every year from the age of five, her mother encouraged her to paint a scene depicting the most significant event in her life that year. The paintings are underneath the line marking her growth in height. Even without the marker displaying her inches of growth, the viewer would know from the gradual improvement in the progression of talent that the artist is more experienced. Standing as though a statue, she studies each scene, reminiscing. The first scene is stick figures of her family with a rainbow over their heads. After she had finished with the painting, her mother drew a semicircle underneath the family and connected that to the rainbow, telling Gabby about the circle of love that connected them.

Another scene that catches her eye brings an instant smile. When she turned the magical double digit of ten, her father bought her Lady, a chestnut brood mare. God knows how much she loved that horse. Being whimsical, Gabby had painted a crown on the horse's head, as she and Lady won the title of Rodeo Princess together. In those years, she remembered feeling that life could not get any better. Well, that held true until she turned fifteen. Yes, that was the year she had her first crush. Under the stands at the rodeo, Tim planted that first sweet kiss on her lips; only a split second in duration, that kiss was cherished for many years. Then on her sixteenth birthday, she wished to paint the universe. She squealed with delight that evening when the stars on the ceiling came to life, shining brightly through the night with the glow-in-the-dark paint.

This is her room, and it tells her story. At sixteen, she had wished to reach for the stars and in the years that followed, she did. With the support of her family, she had dreams of pursuing her goals: graduating from high school and then heading to college for her art degree. She had had the universe in her hands until the year of Anna's cancer diagnosis. It was as if someone snatched Gabby's dreams away. She was devastated when her mother went to her grave. There are no more scenes painted on the walls or the ceiling. Sorrow had consumed her until she found her voice in painting her Trinity Knot series. Painting had provided a creative way for her to vent her grief, saving her.

Both mentally and physically exhausted from the events of the previous night, she stretches out on the double brass bed and covers up with the afghan she made years before. It certainly is a "piece of art." The double-crochet-stitched pattern was originally meant to be a square; however, it ended up having the appearance of a misshapen pentagon. There are some rows with dropped stitches followed by some rows with added ones. Just looking at it makes her smile, but that wasn't always the case.

When Gabby, then a young teenager, first realized her crafting errors, she was so frustrated, she cried and threw the blanket into the garbage. However, the next morning, she found her failed attempt—sorry excuse for a blanket—on the back of the breakfast room chair, while overhearing her mother praising her efforts over the phone. Anna kept this afghan on her bed until she took her last breath. That very evening and many thereafter, Gabby cuddled with that blanket, cherishing it as never before.

With this afghan, her mother had taught her a valuable lesson without ever saying a word: don't be afraid to make mistakes, and thank God for the opportunity to learn and move forward. Gabby had made many beautiful, square afghans since then, each with perfect, even sides; however, her mother favored her daughter's first attempt.

Now, she snuggles the blanket up to her chin, enjoying its softness, breathing in deeply, trying to find her mother's scent in its fibers. Within minutes, much-needed sleep overtakes her.

She is frantic as she runs down the narrow hallway searching for someone ... but who, she isn't sure. She just knows she needs to find him. The rooms are filled with people, but as she searches each face, she only finds strangers. Careful not to miss a room, she continues down the hallway searching as panic overtakes her. Suddenly, she approaches a room, hearing familiar voices. This must be where he is, she thinks, relieved that the craziness will cease. While entering the room, the voices are so loud ...

Gabby awakens startled and notices her rapid breathing. Taking a deep breath and letting it out slowly through pursed lips, she realizes it was a dream, but even though she is awake now, she still hears voices.

Outside her bedroom window, which faces the front of the ranch house, she recognizes her father's deep, authoritative voice giving directions for the bunkhouse used by the workers. As she regains all her senses, she remembers that she is at the ranch for the barbecue. She is grateful for the nap but is also grateful to escape the panic her dream has produced within her.

In addition to her father's voice, she hears another familiar voice. She jolts out of the bed and pushes back the curtain to verify with her eyes what her ears are hearing. Even though his hat prevents her from seeing that dimpled face, she recognizes his toned, muscular body and accompanying gestures. It is Brett!

Her heart skips a beat as her mind questions, *How in the world did Brett get here?* She feels conflicted—is her nervousness joy or regret? While her gaze is set on Brett, she doesn't notice her father's eyes dancing between her and the cowboy.

Breaking the silence and startling Gabby, Wayne King says, "Hello, darlin'." Within a split second, Brett is also staring up at the window.

If she could have hidden, she would have, but it is already too late. Scolding herself for not standing further away so as not to be noticed, she yells back, "Hello, Daddy. How are you?"

Not taking his eyes off her, Brett speaks before King can answer. "Well, hello, Gabby!" he says, tipping his black hat in her direction. With the sun gleaming down on his brown curls and deep tan, Gabby can hardly believe the transformation from tennis pro to model cowboy. He stands below her window flashing his boyish grin. A long awkward silence follows.

Gabby sees her father's eyes dart from her to the young man standing beside him. King breaks the silence. "Seems this young man is an experienced horseman. He has just proven that from our short ride this afternoon."

Gabby, still staring and feeling rather uncomfortable, makes some lame excuse about needing to freshen up and leaves the two men gazing up at the empty window. "Oh, my God," are the only words she can breathlessly manage as she steadies herself, using the bed as a brace. "Brett here and with my dad," she gasps. "I didn't realize that they knew each other."

On one hand, she has a fear of Brett but on the other, she finds herself strangely attracted to him. He is intriguing with his edgy bad-boy demeanor combined with moments of intense vulnerability. This forms mystery, spinning an intricate web. If not careful, she is sure she will get tangled, lured by his deep emerald eyes, brilliant smile, and that amazing sex appeal that she experienced last night. Always hoping to find the best in people is part of her fascination with Brett as she thinks of him as a rare faceted jewel that needs polishing.

Today, she learns he is an accomplished rider—another facet but one that brings her a smile. Why did he fail to mention that he was invited to the barbecue at the dance last night? She has so many questions, but the answers will have to come later as she is running out of time. The shindig is fast approaching.

Gabby is excited about it because this is her favorite event held at the ranch. All the neighbors, ranch hands, and friends, both new and old, will attend. Thinking of friends brings both Ella and Richard to the forefront of her mind. Richard has a standing invitation but after their scene on the dance floor, maybe he will consider her feelings and decide not to come, although she knows in her soul it isn't in his personality to do the logical and practical thing. Sure as a bee is drawn to honey, he will be drawn to the barbecue. In fact, his hunger for business success is one in a line of several difficulties in their relationship. She is certain Richard will be there, hoping to generate business with the wealthy neighbors, who, like King, made their fortunes in the precious black liquid under their land.

Her mind switches from Richard to thoughts of Ella. Like Richard, Ella also loves coming to the ranch to promote her business; however, she also promotes her personal life. More years than Gabby wishes to remember, Ella has ended up with a cowboy in her bed. Ella enthusiastically lives by the motto "You only live once." Even though she is bright and energetic, when it comes to men all logic seems to go by the wayside. Painfully, Gabby has learned to keep her motherly advice to herself. Time and time again, Ella faithfully has run to her for a shoulder to cry on when a relationship shattered.

From a distance away from the window, Gabby cannot help but steal another look at the two men, still engaged in serious conversation. She is still trying to figure out how Brett and her dad know one another. What can they possibly be chatting about with such earnestness? Seeing them together is comforting. Maybe her father can provide a positive influence on Brett just as he has with many of the young men he has employed on the ranch over the years. As the owner of a large spread, he employs many a young, restless man who has needed a little guidance. King can tame the defiant streak in the wildest of horses, so taming a ranch hand in comparison is easy, using these same God-given skills.

Earlier, in the wee hours of the day, the first in a long procession of catering trucks rolled through the gates. Their cargo included tables and chairs, risers needed for building a stage for the band, and many decorations to create a festive air. Food trucks will bring in side dishes to accompany the succulent meats that are roasting in the smoker, along with kegs of beer and cases of soda. The party is always a grand affair, and King spares no expense in making his barbecue the most talked-about get-together in the hill country. Already the rich smell of roasting meats permeates the air. The chicken and beef will be served with beans, potatoes, coleslaw, and piping hot biscuits right out of the King kitchen.

Bales of hay are set around the stage for seating, and strings of colorful lights are draped from pole to pole, creating a festive dance area. The weather forecast is perfect for the event—a cloudless sky with temperatures in the high seventies, slightly atypical for February but a welcome surprise. There is only a slight breeze, so high winds are not going to stop the fireworks that are scheduled for after dusk.

Wayne King and Gabby both love fireworks but for very different reasons. King loves playing with fire, simple but true, and he also enjoys the loud boom. She, on the other hand, enjoys the mingling of the numerous sparks, creating a painting across an otherwise black sky. For the past two years, fireworks were banned in the hill country, as there was a persistent drought; however, the winter's rain offered a surplus, allowing the ban to be lifted.

Gabby can hear Jamie hustling in the kitchen and barking orders to the catering staff there to help serve the dinner. The smell of the secret family recipe for the barbecue sauce fills the air, along with the smell of the freshly baked biscuits.

A few guests from the neighboring ranches have already started arriving. Gabby is sure she heard Richard's Ferrari, a gift he gave himself when he was named a partner at the law firm, come through the gate and up the drive some time before. She is dreading their initial meeting, as she knows there will be ugly words. She wants this evening to be free of stress. Rolling her eyes, she knows that Richard will play the victim card to anyone willing to lend him an ear. He will corner her father and offer excuses for his actions, including those of stress with his work and God only knows what else. It is not uncommon for Richard to avoid responsibility. She had better brace herself. Even though he plays around, he will put up a good fight to keep their relationship going. Now she knows she cannot trust him with her heart. However, the harder she tries to push him away, the tighter he seems to hold on.

Seeing Richard will be inevitable, but for now, she needs to concentrate on getting herself together to meet their guests. She dresses in her western best—jeans, a pink-cream-and-gold plaid shirt, and a brown-fringed vest with matching brown leather boots and belt. The mirror reflects the silver buckle that has the insignia of the King ranch carved into the precious metal. Gabby lifts her hair up in the fashion of a ponytail but decides to let her long, blond hair hang free, and she happily skips down the stairs. She wants to offer warm greetings to Jamie and the house staff and to find her father before more of the guests occupy his time.

After Gabby greets Jamie in the kitchen, her offers to help are refused, and she is shooed away. However, Jamie mentions that her father is eager to speak with her. Approaching the double wooden doors to his study, she pauses for a moment to listen, as she does not wish to interrupt if he is in a meeting.

Her timid knock is followed by her father's warm voice. Opening the door, she quickly stops in her tracks. Her father is seated behind his large wooden oak desk, and sitting in the brown ribbed leather chair is none other than Richard, holding an old-fashioned glass. The two men are sharing some whiskey, and if her instincts are right, it isn't the first pour that remains in their vessels.

"Hello, darlin'. I have been eagerly waiting to see you," says her father, rising from his chair to give her a hug. "You are as beautiful as ever."

"Oh, Daddy, you always say that," she quips after giving him a bear-sized embrace.

"Yes, I do, and I always will, because it is true," he says.

Richard finishes his whiskey during this exchange and stares at them, his eyes looking over the rim of his frames.

Noticing Richard's stare and silence, Gabby awkwardly says, "I can come back if you are busy."

"Nonsense," her father chimes.

Richard gets up from his chair and pours himself another shot of the potent golden liquid, glares at Gabby with detest, and speaks in a matter-of-fact business tone. "You should stay. We would love your input. Your father and I have been speculating about your future. It is only fitting you arrive in time to defend and justify your actions from last evening. You should know that I asked your father for your hand in marriage."

A smug look rests on Richard's face accompanied by an upturned grin. He is clearly pleased with himself. Gabby wants to slap him. She restrains from any physical contact, but she is unable to hide her rage, even here, in her father's presence.

"I don't need to defend my actions to anybody. I thought I made it pretty clear last night that you and I are finished. There is nothing more to discuss," she boldly announces, turning to gaze out the window to avoid facing either man.

Richard starts in again, using the term of endearment that she only wishes to hear from her father, "Well, darlin', last night you seemed pretty involved with that low-life tennis pro. I thought you had better sense than taking up with the likes of him. I know you're angry with me because I was late for the ball, so I'm willing to forgive you for this lapse in judgment. When you act on impulse, you tend to make poor decisions. It is something you will have to work on in the future. Your father will agree with me that our relationship can be quite beneficial for both of us."

"Now hold on there, Richard," says King. "I learned long ago never to make a decision until hearing both sides of a story. I haven't had a chance to speak with Gabby on this matter, but I will not sit here and have you talk about my daughter in that tone. She is an intelligent woman, and just because the two of you fail to see eye to eye doesn't mean she is making a poor decision. I'm beginning to understand more about your relationship." He stands.

"And that low-life tennis pro you were referring to is a guest at my ranch. While here, you will treat him with respect. If that's too much to ask, Richard, you are free to leave. Brett and I had a good ride this afternoon—fine horseman. More than I can say for your past performances, so let's quit the name-calling, shall we? Every man has his own special talents. You are out of line," King scolds.

Quickly, Richard retracts his prior statement, looking down at his glass. "Sir, I apologize. I'm not at my best. I admit I am distraught over

Gabby's refusal of my proposal. My intention is to make amends, not continue this foolishness."

Gabby responds, "Really, Richard, are you sure you want to discuss 'us' in front of my father? Do you really want him to know the real you?"

King jumps in quickly. "Gabby, in all fairness, I probably know more about Richard than you give me credit for. He isn't the first ambitious attorney I've had the pleasure of dealing with."

Gabby continues to explain. "Daddy, I turned down Richard's marriage proposal last night. I cannot overlook his blatant infidelity. His promises are cheap and without merit. He is here vying for your empathy, elevating himself by putting others down." Turning to face Richard, she continues, "Brett may not be the perfect gentleman, but he's ... he's ..." She is suddenly at a loss for words. She hates when she stutters. It makes her look and feel like a fool.

Richard, clearly enjoying her struggle, pressures her more. "Go on, Gabby. What is Brett exactly? My curiosity is piqued. It's a joke for Brett to think he and I are in the same league. And if he does, he is a fool. Besides, everyone can see that you belong to me."

She is dumbfounded, listening to his flawed rhetoric, and is momentarily at a loss for words. Nervously, she turns to her father, gesturing for him to save her from this humiliation. King looks amused from behind his desk. Using silence once again as a tactical maneuver, King scratches his chin as if trying to figure out this little love-hate triangle between Brett, Richard, and his daughter.

Gabby turns abruptly and stomps out of the study, leaving the doors wide open.

CHAPTER 15

Gabby fakes a smile. The barbecue is starting, and she has work to do, so she puts her troubles with Richard and Brett on the back burner. Getting lost in the crowd, she lets all her prior emotions vanish. She assumes her mother's role as the matriarch of the King ranch, standing next to her father, greeting each guest on arrival. She not only enjoys being back on the ranch, but she also enjoys all of the people. The air is festive with the band playing and the hum of people chatting and laughing while they eat and drink. Being united with neighbors and childhood friends brings out the best in Gabby. She is happy, and the glow she exudes is noticeable to all.

It is within a split second, when her eyes meet with Ella's as Ella reaches the Kings in the welcoming line, that her joy is stolen. Immediately, Gabby senses that something is haunting her best friend.

Usually Ella is fun-loving and free-spirited, but tonight there is a more reserved soul with an entitled air.

Cautiously, Ella leans in toward Gabby and whispers softly in her ear, "We need to chat and soon."

The serious tone of her voice confirms Gabby's initial assessment. In drama class, Ella could easily win the vote for best performance, but this is different. This is real; something is terribly wrong. The girls exchange one last look before Ella moves along, giving Wayne King a big hug and kiss. He knows how to lavish compliments on the ladies, and his sweet talk puts an instant smile on Ella's troubled face. Gabby knows she will need to seek out her friend later that evening.

Laughter and gaiety fill the warm night air. A well-known local band's sound encourages dancing with a few pop and rock 'n' roll songs among the two-step country tunes. The stars appearing overhead tell Gabby she has lost all track of time and that a few hours have passed since she first started greeting guests, welcoming them to the ranch. The pit in her stomach reminds her that she hasn't eaten since breakfast. While making her way to the buffet table, she feels a hand on the small of her back followed by a warm nuzzle near her right ear. She turns quickly, knocking the beer out of Brett's hand, spilling the frothy, cool liquid all over his jeans.

"Hey, I waited a lifetime in that line to get this, and you just spilled half of it," he jokes with a twinkle in his eyes.

"Oh, I am so sorry," she says, glancing down at the wet blue fabric to avoid looking up at him.

"I am going to make it my goal to teach you how to relax. You are strung so tight," Brett says. "If I played with a tennis racquet strung as tightly as you, it would seem as if I had the power of a timid little girl. Really, Gabby, geez."

"I am really sorry about your jeans," she says once again, adding, "You can't sneak up on a person like that."

He turns to face her. "I did call your name, but with all of the noise, it's impossible for you to hear."

"What?" she yells, laughing. "I can't hear you. What are you saying?"

He shrugs his shoulders and places his hand on the small of her back again, guiding her through the masses and following closely. The crowd at the buffet table has thinned. Gabby fills her red plastic plate with the succulent meats and special sauce. Brett carries two Solo cups filled with beer, motioning her away from the tables to a hay bale farther from the dance floor, so they can have a conversation without screaming.

After sitting, he offers a toast. "To new beginnings!"

Gabby looks into his face, melting on the inside, and is mesmerized by his boyish grin.

"Hey, it's bad luck not to drink after a toast. That'll make my toast void. Lord knows we can use a fresh start," Brett says.

"I'm sorry," she says again as she takes a sip of her beer and feels its coolness hit her empty stomach.

"Please stop apologizing. Relax. Do you ever let your guard down?" Brett asks.

She cannot contain her muffled laugh. "That's so ironic coming from you," she says. "From the guy who raped me."

"Ouch, that hurts," he exclaims. "I guess I'm the one who needs to keep apologizing. I never meant to hurt you. I misread some signals. I said I was sorry. If I could erase that day, you know I would. But I can't, I can only show you moving forward that I'm not that guy. I am not who you think I am. I'm hoping we can move forward, to new beginnings, as I toasted. Start over. I would really like to. Can we?" He looks at her, pleading, earnestly waiting for an answer.

She hates that she keeps reminding him of that day on the court. In her dreams, she and Brett have started over, and she has forgiven him a million times. But here, sitting next to him within arm's reach, she has to be cautious and firm. It's no wonder he is confused as to the standing of their relationship. Wasn't it just last night, on the balcony, that they shared a kiss? Aware that she is sending mixed signals, maybe, just maybe in the past, she did send similar signals confusing him and giving him the wrong idea.

Brett, aware that she is staring off into the distance in another world, asks, "Hey, where are you, pretty lady?" He snaps his fingers, stirring her away from her thoughts. Then he continues, staring into her brown eyes. "You are such a puzzle, a beautiful puzzle. You never answered my question, can we start over?"

Jolted from her thoughts, Gabby lets her eyes meet his, and with a shy smile, she softly replies, "Of course we can start over. To new beginnings." She touches her cup to his and takes a drink.

He looks away and takes a swig too. "To new beginnings," he says.

Little does he know, in Gabby's mind, he is already exonerated. After their dance and shared kiss, he occupies every one of her thoughts almost every waking minute.

She takes another sip of beer as she looks at the band. They are playing, but she doesn't hear; their song is overshadowed by her feelings about Brett. If she is going to start dating him, there are so many avenues to contemplate, such as how would she fare in a breakup, and will she be just another conquest for the dashing tennis pro? But most importantly, can she trust him? She thought she could trust Richard and that isn't turning out well for her. She feels the warmth of Brett's body, and she inches away. It is hard for her to focus. Does he hear her heart pounding? Why does she make bad choices? Will this be another bad decision if she continues to encourage him and spend time with him?

She takes a deep breath and sighs. She misses her mother most at times like this—even though Anna was a practical woman and would often advise Gabby to wait, as many situations, like a wrinkle in microfiber fabric, will iron themselves away. This situation is not one of those. This is a pressing concern, and waiting is not an option. She needs some sound advice soon.

Since her mother can't give her advice, perhaps she needs to talk to her daddy. He makes multiple important business decisions every day. Maybe it is time to seek his advice. She is aware that if she chooses to involve her daddy and ask his advice, she had better hope she agrees with his opinion. She will have to be clever and not reveal anything about the actual rape because she isn't sure how her daddy will handle that situation.

If she is unable to resolve her own conflict over what happened between her and Brett, how can she possibly explain it to her father? She will just tell him about the extreme changes in Brett's personality, asking her father if he has noticed them too.

Thinking of her father makes her remember to start probing Brett with questions about his relationship with her dad. With all the business and excitement of the day, she has forgotten. Looking at him in the most matter-of-fact way she can manage, she rapidly fires two questions without giving him a chance to respond after the first. "How is it that you know my father? And why didn't you tell me you were coming to the ranch last night?" She forces a large bite of the brisket into her mouth giving him time for a complete answer. She slowly chews, not daring to look at him as he explains.

Clearing his throat, he answers, "Oh, your father ... I just met him last night at the bar. He saw my boots and bolo tie and asked me about my experience as a cowboy. I told him I grew up on a ranch just north of here. I haven't ridden in over ten years. It was his idea that I come out here, ride, and stay for the barbecue. The ranch is great. I'm glad I came. It reminds me of my upbringing. Your father is an interesting man—he's smart, wealthy, and has an amazing daughter."

Gabby lets the last remark slide and continues with her questions. "Exactly what was your upbringing?"

Brett takes a deep breath before unraveling the threads of his life. "My father was a ranch hand. My mother died in a car accident when I was seven. I only have a faint memory of her. My dad raised me on the ranch, where I learned to ride and work next to the ranch hands, herding and branding cattle, and mending fences. In the beginning, it was a good life until my dad died. If I seem a little rough around the edges, I can blame it on being raised by a group of men out in the hill country.

"I was pretty good at riding and roping and won trophies in the local rodeos."

This last statement spikes her interest, and she leans in a little closer to him. He smiles.

Finishing her plate of food, she stares at Brett. *Who is this guy sitting next to me? He certainly is full of surprises.* She is curious as to what other secrets he is hiding beneath his boyish grin. She is beginning to understand her father's interest in him. Is it pure coincidence that Brett ended up here at the ranch today? Probably, but highly unlikely. She needs to have that talk with her father. She drinks the last of her beer, nodding with a perplexed expression.

Unaware that she has forgotten to hide her amusement, Brett says, "You can close your mouth now. You think I have done nothing but play tennis all my life."

Wishing to hear more, she says, "There's more to you than meets the eye. Tell me."

He looks down sheepishly, flashing his dimpled smile, and declares, "No, that's enough about me for one night. No sense boring you. It's your turn to surprise me. Tell me something about you."

She gets a pass from answering when Ella comes into view, shouting and waving at Gabby. Ella is wearing a short, flared denim skirt with a row of matching blue eyelet lace on the hem. She chose a cream-colored low-cut sweater that accentuates her double-D chest. She completes her outfit with a pair of brown-and-pink tooled-leather boots. Every hot-blooded male gives her an approving nod as she meanders past him.

"There you are. I have been looking all over for you," Ella exclaims to Gabby, catching her breath. When Brett, who initially has his back to Ella, stands and turns to face her, she stops speaking in midsentence. "Brett?" she questions. "I'm shocked to see you here. Wow ... I guess you and Gabby are more involved than I thought."

Gabby says quickly, "Actually, Ella, I didn't know Brett would be here. Seems Daddy invited him." She changes the subject. "You look stunning. I love that skirt and those boots. Are they new?"

She knows that Ella is a sucker for fashion and loves to talk about her newly acquired purchases. Ella takes the bait and starts a soliloquy, in which both Gabby and Brett try to act interested. Finally switching topics, Ella blurts out, "Richard gave me a ride to your ranch in his Ferrari. Today was a perfect day for a ride, especially with the top down. It was heavenly. Surely, he mentioned it. He told me he spoke with you."

"I only saw Richard briefly as he was sharing rounds of whiskey with Daddy in the study. No, I don't recall him mentioning anything about you," Gabby said.

Ella's disappointment is obvious as she forces her bottom lip into a pout. Just then, the band switches from playing a pop song to a country-and-western tune. Instantly, Ella grabs Brett's hand and drags him toward the dance floor. Reluctantly, he allows her to pull him along. Ella calls over her shoulder, "I want to see if this tennis player, who is dressed like a cowboy, can dance the two-step. You don't mind, do you, Gabby?"

Gabby yells, "Please, go ahead. I really need to mingle with our guests."

Brett looks back at Gabby as if to say, "Please, save me." She laughs and shoos him along, waving as she walks toward the crowd.

Before she can take more than a few dozen steps toward the crowd, Richard is by her side. He smells of stale whiskey, and Gabby notices a slight slur in his speech.

"I see you were speaking with Ella," he belts. "What is she spouting off about?"

"Richard, you know she's my best friend. It's only right that she talks to me. She seems pleased you gave her a ride in your Ferrari. It surprises me a little. I didn't think you cared much for her. Offering Ella a ride was very thoughtful."

Richard looks away from her and turns his attention to watch Ella and Brett dance. "They make a great couple, don't you think?" He lifts his glass in the direction of the dance floor and then gestures to Gabby. "I really don't understand why you insist on wasting your time with that low-life."

Not wishing to fuel an argument between them in front of the guests, she remains silent. Without warning, Richard takes this opportunity to wrap his arms around her and snuggles his nose into the side of her neck. "You smell great," he coos.

"Let's not make a scene," Gabby says, feeling uncomfortable. She frees herself by gently pushing Richard away, not wishing him to lose his balance in his inebriated state.

"Stop playing games," he says. "Let's make up. I'm tired of fighting."

"This is not the time or the place to have this discussion. I need to be with my guests. Why don't you go sleep it off, and we'll talk in the morning," she quips.

"You need to be with me," he says loudly, gripping her arm.

"Being with you is exactly what I don't need," she says defiantly as she struggles to be released from his embrace. "Stop it. You're hurting me."

Richard turns slightly when a hand grips his shoulder, causing him to lean awkwardly. Brett is towering above him. "Is there a problem?" Brett asks, looking at Gabby while still holding on to Richard.

Richard, upon seeing Brett, releases the grip on Gabby's arm. "No problem," Gabby answers.

"Why don't you mind your own business," Richard demands, glowering at Brett.

"The lady seems uncomfortable, so I did the gentlemanly thing and offered assistance. You want to take this around the corner to discuss further?" Brett asks sternly.

"Is that a challenge, Mr. Tennis Pro?" Richard asks.

Before another harsh word is spoken, Wayne King comes between the two young studs, placing his arms around each of their shoulders. With his boisterous laugh, he chimes, "Wonderful party! You'll have enough to eat? There's plenty more. So glad you both came. I know you young people have lots going on these days, and I appreciate you coming out to the ranch to join Gabby and me.

"Time to get those fireworks started. The sun set an hour ago. I waited three long years for this night. Damn drought, kept me away from having fun," King says happily. Looking at Brett, he adds, "Since Richard is likely to lose a few fingers in his drunken state, care to join me?"

"Yes, sir!" Brett enthusiastically replies. The two men amble off into the nearby field across the lane, away from the crowd, where the fireworks were set earlier, waiting for night.

Finding that she is alone on the dance floor and hearing the raised voices, Ella rejoins the group. Gabby is thankful as she does not wish to be alone with Richard. She takes Ella by the hand asking, "Now, what did you want to tell me?"

Ella loops her arm around Richard. He jerks free and heads off toward the house. Ella pouts, yelling after him, "Richard, come back here. We should tell Gabby together."

Richard shakes his head and yells back at the girls, "Coming here was a mistake. I don't want either of you."

"You don't mean that. Richard, come back," Ella pleads.

Gabby searches Ella's face and sees that she is hurt. Spontaneously, Ella bursts into tears, leaning on Gabby for support.

"I'm so sorry, so sorry," she sobs as the tears stream down her face.

Gabby, who previously was totally in the dark, starts putting the pieces of the puzzle together. Still holding her best friend, she listens to Ella's confession.

She does not even have to ask the question as Ella blurts out, sobbing, "I thought I meant something to him. We had an incredible time last night. He wanted me, and I really needed him to want me. Richard was hurt by your rejection, and he saw you and Brett dancing on the patio. We both saw you, Gabby. You know I wanted Brett. Why did you take him when you have Richard?" Ella looks up at Gabby as more tears roll down her cheeks.

She continues, "Richard asked you to marry him. He is so handsome and rich." Earnestly looking at Gabby, she says, "Gabby,

I wanted to be you. Guys always want you. I wanted to hurt you. I was so angry that you stole Brett from me. I would take Richard in a heartbeat. I slept with him, Gabby. I slept with Richard. I thought we were great together," she repeats, looking at Gabby as if hoping to see shock and anger. "You have everything, and I have nothing. I am tired of always coming in second to you. Now, I feel so foolish. I hate my life."

Gabby pats her friend on the back, doing her best to console her while trying to put the pieces of the puzzle in their proper places. She starts counting: first, Richard asks her to marry him; second, she and Brett are on the patio; third, Richard and Ella see them kissing; fourth, Richard and Ella go spend the night together. The puzzle is piecing together, but she appreciates nothing about it. *That scoundrel. He sleeps with my best friend and then has the nerve to come to the ranch and speak with my daddy, asking Daddy for my hand in marriage. Richard has no conscience and thinks nothing at all about what he does to others. He is totally all about Richard!* She puts her hands on her hips and bites her lip. She vows to have nothing more to do with him.

With all these thoughts going through her mind, she is not aware that Ella has stopped crying and that the loud noise she hears is the start of the fireworks. Gabby looks up as the long-anticipated fireworks fill the night sky. As she searches the sky with all the bright, festive colors, she whispers a prayer to God, praising him and thanking him for showing her Richard's true character. She also sends a prayer up for the friend she holds in her arms, hoping they can repair their friendship and that Ella will heal from her pain. Both girls are better off without Richard, even if that is hard for Ella to see right now.

"Ella, look up at the sky. See how beautiful," Gabby says. Ella wipes her tears with her hand and glances up to the heavens.

Realizing what she just confessed, she repeats, "Oh, Gabby, I am so sorry. Please forgive me. I wasn't thinking straight. Richard used me, and I guess that I used him too."

This day has really taken a strange turn of events. Ella and Gabby stand hugging while watching the rest of the fireworks. They hold hands, enjoying the brilliant twinkling lights in hues of all colors of the rainbow. Gabby smiles, knowing how happy her daddy must be now that he can finally light up the sky. She knows he will be thinking of Anna. The main reason her father wanted the drought to cease was so he could carry on this special family tradition.

She smiles, remembering the good times, standing here in years past with her mother. she has plenty to be grateful for, and at this moment, she is certain she feels her mother's love reaching down from the heavens. Anna loved the sky, but she also loved the land. Anna did her best to pass both down to her daughter. Through all of the turmoil of the day, right now, standing in the open field watching the fireworks, all Gabby feels at this moment is peace.

Ella joins Gabby in saying farewell to the guests, and Gabby appreciates all of their compliments. It seems the evening was a huge success.

Wayne King's boisterous laugh can be heard every so often, so Gabby knows her father is down by the bonfire. The workers and neighboring ranchers, longtime friends of King, are seated on hay bales, drinking the last of the beer while telling jokes and reminiscing of days gone by. She wonders what happened to Brett, as she hasn't seen him since he left with her father to help set off the fireworks. With Ella clinging to her side, Gabby thinks it best not to look for him. She will see him tomorrow.

It is past midnight when the men around the bonfire part ways. Brett is glad for the numbing effects of the alcohol. He knew he had drunk too much when his head spun as it hit the pillow. He lies fully clothed in the upper bed in the bunkhouse. King invited him to ride again in the morning. At the time, it seemed like a good idea, but now he regrets his decision. The sights and smells around him cause an uneasy feeling. Everything reminds him of the life he walked away from fifteen years before. His heart beats faster, and his breathing becomes more rapid. All of his senses are on high alert—the taste of whiskey on his breath, the feel of the wool blanket beneath, the smell of the horses, and the snores of the men sleeping nearby. Images of that dreadful night he was raped come forward. He tries driving the images away with pleasant thoughts of Gabby. It is going to be a long, restless night.

He lies there thinking. The day at the ranch started better than he had anticipated: he was reminded of his love for horseback riding, he enjoyed the barbecue and the fireworks, plus spending time with Gabby was priceless. All these happy moments give way to false thinking, making him believe the lost young teenager is gone and now he, a grown man, can handle being back. He remembers the advice from a fitness article—control your thoughts, control your actions. Begging his breathing to slow, he thinks, *I am in control.*

He also is reminded of the purpose for the trip—getting closer to Gabby. It saddens him that he was unable to break away from King and search for her. He sits up in his bunk and pulls the curtain aside, his eyes following the moonlit road to the ranch house. He is sure he heard Gabby's voice earlier coming from the porch, but he knows it is too bold for him to impose. He will have to wait until morning.

CHAPTER 16

The morning sun is blazing brightly through the open window, beckoning Gabby to say hello to the new day. She squints and stretches. The clock on her nightstand tells her it is after nine a.m. Ella is in the queen bed sleeping next to her. The smells of coffee and bacon waft up the wooden stairs, signaling the girls to come on down for some breakfast.

Gabby nudges Ella. "Hey, girlfriend, time to rise and shine. It's after nine."

"Do I have to?" Ella replies, opening one eye while proceeding to cover her head with the quilt.

Last evening, after the guests left, Gabby grabbed a bottle of expensive cabernet from her father's stash. She and Ella emptied it, rocking on the porch chairs, laughing over events from their college days. They toasted and chatted about professors and sorority sisters, laughing over stupid boyfriends so loudly they were shooed quiet by Jamie in the wee hours of the morning. Both of them were glad they did not allow Richard or Brett to ruin their friendship, one that was built on so many wonderful times spent together.

The girls wash their faces, comb their hair, and quickly dress before heading downstairs to join the others for breakfast. However, after seeing several dirty dishes on the table, Gabby asks Jamie, "Where's Daddy?"

"You know your father. He is always up at the crack of dawn—out riding with that handsome young man. What's his name ... I just met him yesterday," she says, looking up, testing her memory while clearing the dirty dishes from the table. "It will come to me," she continues. "Brett, yes, that's his name. How could I forget? He was here earlier asking for you. I assured him you would still be here when he returns from his ride. He seems quite smitten with you." Jamie looks up at Gabby to see her reaction.

"Miss Gabby, you and I need to have some girl talk. Whatever happened between you and that lawyer friend of yours? He was in quite a stew last night, throwing his things into his bag, and then he got into that fancy red car of his and took off. He didn't even wait until the fireworks were over." Jamie hesitates, searching Gabby's comfort level with the conversation. "I thought he popped the question, since he came yesterday flashing that beautiful yellow canary diamond ring. Hope I'm not speaking out of turn here." She pours their first cup of coffee.

Gabby looks down and shakes her head side to side. "It wouldn't have worked between us, Jamie." Ella sips her morning java and doesn't dare explain her role in the breakup but just stares at the other two women, listening intently.

Jamie, looking up from her coffee mug, speaks up quickly. "I'm not too sad about it, Miss Gabby. I really didn't care for his high airs. But who am I to judge. I just want you to find someone who will make you happy. You need to start making babies. Your father will make a great granddad. He will be in seventh heaven teaching those kids all about ranching and cattle. He can teach them to ride. It will be nice to have some youngsters around again." She looks up at the ceiling and shakes her head before continuing. "Your father is no spring chicken. Your mother's passing stole some years from him. I want to see him laugh again. He is a good man—one of the best. Well, enough of the lecture. I'm sorry if I overstepped and said too much. You know I love you like a daughter and only want the best for you."

Gabby thanks Jamie for her honesty and assures her again that her rejection of Richard's marriage proposal is the right decision.

Gabby and Ella finish breakfast with conversation about the barbecue the evening before, and then they help Jamie clear the table. Since Richard left last night, Gabby lends Ella her car as Ella needs to get back to town.

"Thanks so much, Gabby," Ella says, hugging her friend. "You are a lifesaver. My boss would be sure to fire me if I didn't show up at work this afternoon."

"No problem," Gabby answers. "I want to hang out here a while. It has been months since I spent time at the ranch. Today is going to be ten degrees above normal, so it will be a great day to hike. Besides,

I need to spend some time with my dad. I'll catch a ride back to town with him."

"You're the best," Ella yells from the open window of the SUV, pressing the gas pedal, tires spinning on the loose gravel.

"Take care of my car and no speeding," Gabby screams, watching her car race down the lane. Even though she enjoyed her time with Ella, she is happy to finally have some time alone.

She watches the car until it is out of sight, and then skips back to the house, planning her day.

CHAPTER 17

Gabby makes some sandwiches from the leftover barbecue meat and stuffs them in her backpack that already holds her sketchbook, pencils, and watercolor paints. She forgot her Canon but is thankful that cell phones can take decent enough photos to capture details that she may not have the time to complete when doing a quick thumbnail sketch. She also grabs some carrots and a few apples as snacks for the horses, as well as some bottles of water.

On a whim, she grabs a flask from the bar, filling it with some vodka. She plans on spending the better part of the day out by the lake. Relaxing on the water's banks and painting seems like a pretty awesome thing to do on her day off. She really needs a vacation, so today is going to be a vacation day.

She walks past the barn and bunkhouse, feeding some of the treats to the horses that stand close to the fence. She notices that her father's prize stud, Monster, is missing. This reminds her that Jamie mentioned at breakfast her father and Brett were out riding. After passing the barn, Gabby turns to follow the narrow path that leads to the creek, which eventually feeds into a lake. The wide-open space lifts her spirits, making her feel free. She recognizes instantly that she misses this feeling with her busy life in town and vows to spend more time in the future at the ranch.

Turning the last bend toward the creek, she hears the heavy tread of horses approaching from the opposite direction.

"Well, Brett, look what we found here ... a lost kitten," her daddy says, smiling mischievously and looking down at her from the saddle of his big brown stallion.

"Hi," Gabby greets them. She shields her eyes from the sun so she can see the two men more clearly. "You got an early start on the day," she chirps happily.

"Your grandpap taught me years ago, and I will do my best to quote him: 'If a man doesn't get half his work done by ten a.m., there is a good chance the other half is left undone.' Brett, what time is it?"

"It's ten-forty a.m., sir," Brett answers in a military tone.

"That late? Heck, there's a good chance I may not finish my work today," King stammers.

While her father is deep in thought about the time of day, Gabby reaches into her backpack and starts feeding treats to both horses. She places an apple in the palm of her hand and offers it to Monster. The stallion wraps his lips around it, snatching the apple from her hand in record time. She laughs out loud, as her father teasingly curses under his breath, "Womenfolk, always spoiling somebody. No one is safe, not even a horse."

King continues, "I need to run and get some work done, but that's no reason to cut your day short. It's the perfect day for a picnic. I'll have Jamie put together a nice lunch for you two. Gabby, I'd really appreciate it if you could show Brett the rest of the ranch. I'll have one of the hands bring you the Jeep so you can four-wheel the entire property. On horseback, we covered less than half."

Gabby pouts, asking, "Daddy, you aren't going back to town today, are you?"

"I'm not going anywhere. I need to talk to Rusty about the fence that's down. I plan to stay a few days. We'll have a nice dinner tonight. I'll be all yours," King promises with a reassuring nod of his head. "Brett, can you stay for dinner? Jamie makes a really nice spread."

"Thanks for the invite, but I really need to get back tonight. I have work early in the morning," Brett explains.

"Suit yourself. If Gabby can change your mind, there's always a chair at the table." King nudges the sides of Monster with his knees while turning him around with the reins.

Gabby is shocked by the wave of disappointment that travels through her after hearing that Brett is leaving today. She was hoping to get to know him better.

As King disappears down the trail behind the trees, Brett hops off his horse, holding the reins in his hand. Gabby notices that Brett seems different here on the ranch. He is more down- to-earth, more relaxed. It seems as if he belongs here.

"So here we are," he says to Gabby, smiling.

"So here we are," she shyly repeats. In silence, they stand looking at each other.

She makes conversation first. "Did you enjoy the barbecue?"

"Yes, it was a perfect evening. Everyone seemed to enjoy themselves."

She agrees, nodding affirmatively up at him. "Let's walk along the creek where it meets the lake just over that ridge. It will be a perfect place for a picnic lunch." She turns toward the path that runs parallel to the creek. Brett follows, leading his horse behind him.

"Hey, why are you walking when you can be riding?" he asks quizzically. Then he adds, "I've been riding all morning. To be honest with you, my butt is sore. I rode yesterday and now this morning and, well, I'm just not used to it. Let's see how you look on a horse. Clearly, growing up on the ranch, you can ride. Show me."

Gabby turns and relishes the idea of riding. She hasn't been on a horse since early last fall. "Oh, I can ride. No doubt about that. How fast can you walk?" she inquires, smiling at Brett.

She walks up to Frog, the brown quarter horse with a white blaze on his forehead, and puts her left foot into the stirrup. Swinging her right leg up over the saddle, she feels a firm hand on her butt. Slightly irritated, she glares at Brett. "I can do it myself."

"Just want to be helpful. Truth is, I just couldn't resist with your big ass in my face," he says, smiling.

Gabby turns several shades of red, and then pipes in an unfriendly tone, "So that's why you want me to ride."

Once again, he defends his actions and says, "Hey, it was harmless ... really, Gabby." Then he proceeds. "You give such mixed signals. Is it my imagination gone wild or did we share a moment on the patio at the dance? I thought you wanted me to touch you. You are so confusing."

He looks up at her with his puppy-dog eyes, and suddenly Gabby is ashamed. She is acting like a schoolgirl, not the polished, mature woman she wants the world to see. But this isn't the world, this is Brett. She did want him to touch her. Well, at least a little. What harm is there in one kiss? Closing her eyes and flipping his cowboy hat back so as not to hit the brim, she leans down, and her lips brush against his ever so lightly.

"I'm sorry," she says sweetly, allowing their eyes to meet. The kiss lasts just a split second, but it seems to make everything between them all right. Aware that her heart is pounding and that a nervous tremor makes her mouth twitch, she prays Brett has not noticed.

He seems mesmerized by this unanticipated act of kindness and is speechless. He turns and starts leading Frog along the path while Gabby sits upright in the saddle. Now it is her turn to look at his butt!

They meander along the creek in silence, enjoying the sounds of nature. The birds sing overhead and the sounds of the water rippling downstream create a background harmony. The sun is coming out in full force, and the temperatures have soared into the eighties. King was right once again—it is the perfect day for a picnic.

After a short distance, they come to the point in the trail where the creek runs into the small lake. Adjacent is an open field. The first signs of the Texas bluebonnets scatter over the meadow. Gabby cannot resist the temptation to ride. She kicks Frog hard with her knees and yells, "Let's go!" And off they gallop into the meadow. Brett watches as she rides the steed, sailing through the air with her hair flowing in the wind.

She hears the sound of the Jeep before she sees Rusty stop near Brett. They shake hands. Pulling the reins hard to the left, she and Frog return, stopping abruptly close to where the men are standing. She dismounts quickly, passing the reins to Rusty.

"Watching you ride is a sight for sore eyes. We've missed having you around here," Rusty says.

She goes over and gives him a hug. "I've missed you and Jamie too. I need to make coming out here more of a priority." Rubbing her chin, she adds, "I believe it has been since the beginning of fall, last year."

Still looking at Gabby, Rusty replies, "Your dad wanted me to trade the Jeep for Frog and here ..." He stops in midsentence as he reaches into the passenger seat of the Jeep. "I brought you lunch. Bet you can't guess what tasty morsels are hidden in here," he says with a wink. Then he adds, "I did see Jamie put a surprise in there. Make sure you dig to the bottom."

Frog finds the bucket of water that Rusty had placed on the ground without the need for an invitation. Rusty allows him to drink his fill before mounting and yells, "Have fun. The tank is full."

Finding they are alone once again, Gabby says, "Well, here we are." She breathes in deep.

"Yes, here we are," Brett repeats and then adds, "again."

Gabby reaches for the picnic basket and lifts the lid. "No surprises here, barbecue," she says, laughing. "Grab the cooler and blanket. We'll set up in the shade of that old oak next to the lake," she calls over her shoulder. After walking to the tree, she turns to Brett. "This is as perfect a place as any for lunch. You hungry?" she asks.

"Starved," he answers.

Gabby helps him spread the blanket in the shade of the oak and sets down the basket and the cooler on the lower corners. The first hints of bluebonnets cover the bank of the lake, their scent barely recognizable. Brett plops down on the brightly colored granny square quilt and opens the cooler, taking out two bottles of sparkling lemonade. He opens them, offering one to Gabby. She reaches for the bottle and smiles while reaching for her backpack.

"I can make this a bit more interesting," she says as she takes a swig of the lemonade and pours some vodka from her flask into the rest of the bottle.

She offers her flask to Brett, and he does the same. "You are a bad girl ... drinking before noon. Who would have guessed? I hope your dad knows that it was his little princess who brought the hard stuff, trying to get me tipsy so she can take advantage of me."

"I'm not a bad girl, just relaxing while having a picnic on a beautiful day," she replies.

He lifts his bottle and clanks it against hers. "To new beginnings," he toasts, seemingly searching her eyes for approval.

"To new beginnings," she repeats back in a whisper, avoiding his stare and thinking *déjà vu*.

They share more small talk about the barbecue as they enjoy the contents of the basket, especially the chocolate chip cookies hidden near the bottom.

"Jamie bakes the best cookies," Gabby says with a mouthful of the treat. Embarrassed for talking with her mouth full, she shyly looks at Brett, offering her apology, "I'm sorry."

At that moment, he lifts his hand to her lips. "A crumb," he says playfully and flicks it away as he leans in and kisses her. His kiss is gentle and sweet but playful with a bit of caution. Her response is reserved. She does not want to seem anxious for his affection, but she also does not want to deny him. Inside, she is smiling and excited but also conflicted. She hasn't yet resolved the ambiguity she feels toward him.

Breaking away from him, she asks, "Did you enjoy the fireworks?"

As if amused with the change in topic, he answers in a matter-of-fact tone, grinning and looking at Gabby smiling. "It was pretty awesome. Your dad really gets into it. First time I ever got to light them. It's scary at first but fun. How about you? You have fun watching them with Richard?"

She answers, trying her best to match his sarcastic tone. "Oh, yeah, drunk Richard. That was lots of fun, along with weeping Ella. They are quite the pair. Seems they left the ball together. Ella thought it was the start of a relationship, but it turns out Richard was using her." She continues, "Jamie tells me Richard drove back to town last night. He really should not have been driving."

"And Ella?" Brett inquires.

"Ella needed a shoulder to cry on. When it comes to men, she doesn't have much luck."

"But Richard was your choice first," Brett reminds her.

"Yes, I know," she admits. "Daddy thought we would be good

together, but Richard turned out to be … let's just say very ambitious to get to the top, and his greed took control."

"You always do what Daddy wants?"

"No, not always," she says, teasingly hitting his arm. "However, Daddy is a wise man. When I do ask his advice, he is usually right."

"What will your daddy say about me?" Brett asks, leaning back to get her expression. "You threatened me, using your dad as your strong arm, remember?"

She stares at him. Then she answers, "Truthfully, I haven't asked him. In fact, if my daddy ever found out what you did to me, we would not be sitting here together having a picnic. I can say that with all certainty."

"Are you going to tell him?" he asks, lowering his eyes.

"I hope it never comes up." She pauses and says, thinking out loud, "He would think me crazy to ever trust you."

He shakes his head and looks down. "Gabby, we have been over this so many times. I thought we put the past in the past, new beginnings, remember?"

Switching the topic of the conversation, she says, "I'm still confused as to how you got invited to the ranch. It seems like you are my daddy's new best friend. Tell me, how and when did this happen?"

Brett, shaking his head, dutifully answers, "As I told you before, I met your father at the bar two nights ago at the country club. He invited me. Do you wish I wasn't here?" He looks into her eyes.

"You intrigue me," she finally says.

"You didn't answer my question."

"How is it that I ask you a question and you answer it by asking me a question? Maybe you are not the person I should be asking. I should be asking my father why he invited you here." She goes on. "Brett, you're a player. I am not. So why are you here?"

He repeats after her, "Why am I here? Okay, I'm here because, one, like I said before, your dad invited me; two, I grew up on a ranch riding, and I haven't done that in a long time and thought it would be fun; three, because I like you and want to get to know you. I want to see where you grew up. I think it might help me understand you."

Gabby is shocked by his well-thought-out response and openness. She answers him honestly. "Things are pretty complicated, Brett. It seems Richard came here yesterday to ask my dad for my hand in marriage. Since I turned him down, I guess he thought he could convince my dad that it would be a benefit for us to get married."

Hearing the *M* word makes Brett sit up straighter. He raises his eyebrows and asks her, "What did your dad say to that?"

"Daddy said he needs to hear both sides of the story. With the barbecue and all the guests, we haven't had a chance to talk," she confesses.

Brett takes her hand in his, asking, "What do you want, Gabby?"

She gazes up at him and answers, "I don't want Richard, if that's what you are asking."

"What about us? Have you thought about dating me?"

"Like I said earlier," she restates, "you're a player. I'm not. Go play with someone else."

"You really don't mean that," he says, pushing her down on the blanket, trapping her with his arms on either side of her head. "I kind of like playing with you." His face is only inches from hers.

She feels vulnerable and dizzy. He moves closer, and her eyes close. She has no words left. Her body is on autopilot. Brett tips off his cowboy hat and kisses her. Finding no protest, he kisses her again, this time more passionately. She responds by arching her back, pulling him closer. His arms reach around her, and he playfully cups her breast. His taste is sweet and spicy. His tongue eagerly finds her own, and she is lost in his kiss, lost in his touch, and lost in the moment.

In the midst of their passion, they are interrupted by the spilling of the lemonade bottles. "Look what you did," he says, laughing. "You spilled the lemonade, so now we'll have to drink straight vodka."

Gabby laughs as she sits up. "Oh, well, too bad for us." She finds the flask and takes a swig before handing it to him. Grabbing her sketchpad and pencils from her backpack, she orders Brett to sit still so she can draw his portrait. He places his hat back on his head and sits up straight, staring at the lake.

"Is this good?" he asks, flashing a grin, making his dimple more pronounced.

"Great. You'll need to sit perfectly still," she teases with the pencil in her hand, "or you will be disappointed that I didn't capture you correctly."

After ten minutes have passed, Brett turns to her, trying to catch a glimpse of her work. She quickly hides her tablet and remarks, "You'll get to see it soon enough."

After a few more minutes, he cannot wait another second. She is totally immersed in her drawing. He grabs her pad. There is no sketch of him but a nice drawing of the tree and bluebonnets with the lake in the background. "You liar," he yells, shaking his head. "You get me to sit here like a statue and you're sketching bluebonnets!" He pouts, sticking out his lower lip.

She laughs and laughs, as he actually seems to have his feelings hurt. "If you knew about my artwork, you would know that I don't draw or paint portraits!"

"You know what happens to little girls who get caught in a lie? They get punished," he says jokingly. With that, he pulls her down over to his lap and places his hand on her bottom. "This is going to hurt me more than it's going to hurt you." Teasingly he slaps her butt.

Gabby, not to be manhandled, finds his arm and sinks her teeth into his skin, giving him a delicate bite. Surprised by her action, he says, "So you want to play rough?" She can feel his firm muscles as he flips her over to face him, continuing to hold her down. "You know, I'll win."

Yes, she is well aware that he will win. He has won in the past, and the memory of that day on the tennis court floods into her mind. She pushes against him to no avail. She can feel her heart racing, causing an audible beating in her ears. She knows her breathing is heavy. Her fear of being confined by the man who raped her is causing her to panic. All of those feelings she thinks she has tucked away come forward once again—that dark cloud, that veil of fear. She hoped she would be stronger. But at this moment, the panic and feelings of defeat are so intense, she struggles and demands, "Let me go."

"I'll let you go for now," he says playfully.

Not wishing him to know the full extent of her anxiety, Gabby quickly jumps up and starts clearing the remnants of their picnic. He must feel that the vibrations that were once playful have turned into a more serious air. She throws the basket and blanket into the back of the Jeep. Following her lead, Brett does the same with the cooler.

"I'm driving so you're riding shotgun," she yells to him. She wipes away beads of sweat that have formed on her brow. She wishes she could wipe away her fears just as easily. Thankful she is back in control, she feels her panic and fear slowly dissipating.

Brett grabs a bottle of lemonade from the cooler, opens it, and drinks it in one large gulp. Gabby watches and once again soaks in his good looks. In her fantasies, a thousand times over she allows him to kiss and touch her. Realizing her fear of the sexual assault has resurfaced, she takes a slow deep breath, reminding herself that he has apologized and has been so kind to her these past few months. She reminds herself that she has forgiven him and has flirted with him, encouraging his advances. God, she is pathetic. However, forgiveness is not the same as forgetting. Maybe she should see a therapist. This thing is bigger than she wants to believe. It is a monster hiding in her mind—one she is having difficulty controlling. Brett must think her a crazy, foolish girl. Does she want that? No! It is all so confusing.

Hours pass like minutes as they drive the Jeep to the four corners of the ranch. She has not seen some parts of the ranch in the last few years, and she is actually enjoying the tour. She shows Brett the countless acres of longhorn cattle grazing on the eastern perimeter. They drive to the far end of the lake to the north. They find the dozen oil derricks to the west. They stop in the wetlands to the south. At this point, Gabby jumps out of the driver's seat. Glancing over at Brett, she says, "It's your turn, cowboy. Slide on over here. Do you think you can find your way back to the ranch?"

He shoots her a glance as if to say, you've got to be teasing, right? He slides over the bench seat behind the wheel as she takes her place in the passenger's seat. "You had better buckle in and hold on tight," he warns her as he revs up the engine, spinning gravel everywhere.

Brett turns out to be more of a daredevil than she imagined. His driving reminds her of her father's driving when she was younger. Years ago, her daddy delighted in the sound of her squeal. It seemed the louder she screamed, the faster he would drive and the rougher terrain he would find. With Brett at the wheel for the past hour, Gabby's insides are sore. She isn't certain if it is from laughing so much, the many bumps they encounter, or creeks they plow through. Maybe it is a combination of all those things. She sighs with relief when the Jeep finally rounds the path, giving her a view of the ranch house and barn.

When Brett pulls up next to the ranch house, she jumps out of the Jeep. She is beginning to realize just how much dust and mud they have on them. The Jeep also shows signs of a much-needed bath. Wayne King is on the porch rocking with Rusty when the couple covered in mud approach.

"Looks like the two of you had a fun time if your appearance is any indication. Who is going to wash my Jeep?" he asks, following the question with a loud, boisterous laugh.

"Brett managed to find every mud puddle and pothole along the way," Gabby informs the two men while trying to brush the mud off of her blue denim shorts without any success.

Brett holds out his hand. "Thank you, Mr. King, for the visit. I really enjoyed the weekend, but it's time to head back home."

King quickly gets up from the rocking chair. "I wish you would stay. Get cleaned up. Pack your things. Dinner is at the top of the hour. Surely a man's got to eat, so you may as well have one of Jamie's home-cooked meals. You only have a two-hour drive so you will be back in no time."

"Since you put it that way," Brett says, "how can I refuse?"

"Less than an hour! I need to hurry. See you all at dinner," Gabby calls back as she is already reaching for the front door. King puts his arm around his daughter, stopping her, and kisses her on the cheek.

She takes the stairs two by two, nearly crashing into Jamie. "Hey, you're pretty chipper," says Jamie.

"Oh, sorry," Gabby says, then adds, "I didn't mean to run you over."

"Dinner is in an hour. Your father's favorite. Meatloaf and mashed potatoes."

"Sounds wonderful. You're the best," Gabby replies, closing the door to her room.

CHAPTER 18

Gabby glances in the mirror and laughs. She is a sight with mud caked in her hair and on her cheek. She showers and carefully applies her makeup. Replacing her trinity knot necklace around her neck, she thinks of her mother. She seriously wishes to have her mother to confide in at this moment. There are many questions flooding her mind but in the forefront is the ultimate question: can she really develop a meaningful relationship with the man who assaulted her? It does sound crazy.

She carefully chooses her ivory eyelet dress and her navy blue pumps. She allows her hair to hang freely around her shoulders. After spraying on her Chanel perfume, she grabs the trinity knot earrings to complete her outfit, wondering if Brett will notice her wearing them. Pleased with her reflection in the mirror, she leaps down the stairs to enjoy a glass of wine before dinner. She hopes to speak with her father alone. She needs advice from someone who can be objective, but she questions how much of her story she really wants to expose. She feels so conflicted.

On second thought, knowing her dad owns a shotgun and isn't afraid to use it, she changes her mind about confiding in him while Brett is still at the ranch. It may be best not to involve her emotional father. Instantly, it becomes obvious to Gabby that she needs professional advice. Today, the episode with Brett that caused her to panic confirms she still has some open emotional scars. She vows to make an appointment with a therapist first thing Monday morning.

She pours a glass of chardonnay from an already opened bottle in an ice tub on the counter. She smiles at the thoughtfulness of her father. He knows the pleasure they both enjoy from cherished family conversation over a glass of wine on the porch before dinner.

"There you are," King says as he stands and gives her another hug. "I have been eagerly waiting for you!"

"I tried to hurry. Really, I did," she confesses. "We have so much to talk about."

"Yes, we do. How are you?" he asks, holding her hands and gazing into her eyes.

"I'm fine, Daddy."

"Really?" King asks. "So, what is the deal with Richard? I heard his side of the story, and I am anxious to hear what you have to say. I probably can figure it out, but I want to hear it straight from you."

"Daddy, he slept with Ella, just two nights ago ... my best friend. It's disgusting. Then he has the nerve to come here talking about marriage," she replies angrily. She cannot believe the emotions that rage within.

King speaks up quickly, giving Richard some slack. "Yes, he told me as much. He seems torn up about the whole thing. A man can do some pretty stupid things when he is hurting."

Gabby glares at her father, takes a sip of her wine, and in the calmest voice she can manage remarks, "I can hardly believe that you of all people are defending him."

King continues, "People get married for all kinds of reasons: some political, some financial, and yes, some for love. It's rare to get all three in a tidy package wrapped with a nice bow. I said rare, not impossible."

She is confused. Why would her father betray her?

"But with that said, I just want you to be happy," he says. "My greatest wish is for you to find someone to share a lifetime that parallels what I had with your mother. God knows how much I loved her and have missed her."

"I miss her too, Daddy. There is so much I would love to speak with her about." Gabby continues, "I know I'm a hopeless romantic. I want to be happy. I want love, true love. I want someone whom I can trust and someone who will be there for me. You and Mother taught me the importance of family, and family doesn't seem to be important to Richard. Richard has his own ambitions. I am moving on." With those words, she sits back in the rocking chair and stares out at the horizon.

"Fair enough," King says. "Gabby, since we're on the subject of relationships, I have something I want to tell you."

He pauses. "I'm seeing someone."

She reacts with surprise and lots of questions. "You're seeing someone? Who is she? How did the two of you meet? When can I meet her?"

"Whoa, whoa there, kitten," King replies. "I wasn't sure how you would feel about this. I know how close you were to your mother. I can't replace her, Gabby, and I'm not trying to do that. Truth is, I'm lonely. When you have a great relationship and then that person is gone, you're lost. I miss your mother every day, but life goes on. I need to go on. I want to share my life with someone."

Gabby reaches for her daddy's hand and replies, "I understand. Really I do. I want you to be happy." She looks into his eyes and sees his sincerity. She loves this man so much.

"So ... who is this mystery woman?" she asks. Hearing this news from her father pushes all of her conflict over a relationship with Brett to a back corner of her mind.

King says, "I am so relieved that you are okay with this. I invited her to dinner this evening. She got here earlier this afternoon while you were showing Brett the ranch. I wanted to have this talk with you before introducing her."

Gabby is wide-eyed. "She's here now?"

King answers, "Yes, she is!" At that moment, he gets up from the rocking chair and opens the front door, calling into the ranch house, "Jamie, send out our special guest. I want Gabby to meet my lady friend." Holding the door open, he reaches for the approaching woman's hand and in his excitement, yanks her out on the porch.

Gabby's jaw drops as she recognizes her boss. "Rita!" she exclaims. "Daddy, you're seeing Rita?"

"That I am," he replies, giving Rita a Texas-sized hug. He then turns his attention back to his daughter. "You okay with your old man dating your boss?"

She is thrilled, and it is hard for her to contain her overwhelming excitement. She exclaims, "Two of my favorite people in the whole wide world and you're asking me if it is okay? It's more than okay. I think it's great!"

She jumps out of the rocking chair and gives them both a hug. She takes Rita's hands into her own, asking, "How long have you been keeping this from me?"

Rita blushes as she answers, "Only a few months. We danced together at the Christmas party, and it just felt right. It's comfortable and easy. We didn't want to tell you until we were certain we have something worth talking about." King looks from one woman to the other.

Curious still, Gabby asks, "Is it serious?"

Rita replies, "Well, I guess it is officially serious since your daddy has included me in this family gathering."

King jumps into the discussion while putting his arm around Rita's waist. "I really like this little lady. She makes me laugh and smile again. I've missed that." After confessing his love, he pulls Rita closer to him, giving her a peck on the cheek. She stands, gleaming; she lifts her face up to King, and Gabby can feel their shared joy.

With all the excitement among the trio on the porch, they are unaware that Brett has walked up the drive and is witness to the announcement. He remains silent.

Finally, Brett speaks after a break in their conversation, making his presence known. "Looks like a celebration." Rita and King both nod in approval.

Gabby looks at Brett and her pulse races. He really is an Adonis.

His hair neatly curls where the strands reach his white shirt collar. His green eyes dance bright, and his dimple glows against his tan, olive skin. His blue jeans hold their front crease, and his silver buckle reflects the last of the sun's rays. Lastly, his boots, dusty earlier, brag of a recent shine. Waves of his spicy cologne reach her, and she is stunned at the arousal stirring within her. It is obvious that Brett takes pride in his appearance; it is also obvious why he is pursued by so many women. He is gorgeous, and he is standing right here with her. He could have been hers earlier this afternoon, but she turned him away.

She wonders how long he will stick around, knowing her behavior mimics a teasing schoolgirl whenever they are alone. On the blanket by the lake, he had professed his interest in her. How can she make him understand the panic and flashbacks she experiences whenever they are alone? If she confides in him, will he understand, or will he laugh at her and brush off her reaction as silly? Will he be patient and allow her time to work through her feelings? There is only one way to find out. She will have to tell him. If she wants to move forward with Brett, she needs to trust him and put all of her cards on the table. But that will have to come later.

After watching her daddy and Rita holding hands, Gabby has a sudden urge to reach out for Brett. She wishes to feel his strong hands and wonders how they would feel holding on to hers. Will they be comfortable and easy together? She wonders but doesn't dare follow through and execute her plan. He catches her staring at him and turns away quickly.

"Get up here and join us for a toast, Brett. It's an occasion to celebrate. I am so glad you decided to have dinner with us," King says, still holding onto Rita. Brett takes the wine glass from him.

After toasting, they sit on the porch, looking across the vast flatland littered with prickly pear and cedars, watching the sun setting in the horizon. Gabby fights back her feeling of nostalgia as she watches her daddy reach for Rita's hand once more. She watched his same gesture with her mother numerous times. She is happy he and Rita have found each other and with time, she will get used to the idea. It will be good.

She looks to her right at Brett and imagines what a relationship with him would hold for her. There are so many unanswered questions: will she become another number in the long chain of women Brett has already pursued? Can she handle a casual relationship, or will she find true love? Once again, sensing her gaze, he turns to face her and grins; however, this time, she does not look away. His smile is contagious, and she easily smiles back.

His hand reaches up and brushes back her blond hair, exposing her earrings. He casually remarks, "You're wearing them. I like that."

The earrings had been her test, one that Brett easily passed. Pleased that he notices this small detail, she leans toward him, her face just inches from his, and softly whispers as if not to disturb the serenity of the evening, "They are a perfect match to my necklace. Thank you."

He leans forward to steal a kiss but glances up at King, sitting just a few feet away. He takes a slow, deep breath and says, "It's hard for me to control myself around you."

The light brush of his hand against her face also creates an equally unsettled reaction in Gabby. A wave of excitement runs through her body. She has never experienced such an intense attraction to any man before. This is a new feeling for her to discover and explore. It is exciting but scary, knowing the history they share.

"You need to tell me about that necklace you always wear. It seems pretty important to you. Why is that?" Brett whispers back to her.

His stare is more than she can bear, and she turns away, pretending to gaze once again at the remnants of the sunset to the west. She answers in a teasing tone, "If you're really good, someday, maybe, just maybe, I'll tell you about it." She lets out a small giggle as she turns to face him. His dimple deepens slightly as his eyes take on a quizzical look, accepting her statement as a challenge.

Once again, she turns to the horizon in the distance to break the intensity of the moment. They sit in silence, absorbing the first notes of the crickets and frogs. It is another beautiful evening in paradise. The silence is broken by the ringing of the dinner bell. "Hope everyone is hungry. I know I am," King chimes, getting up from his rocker.

As they enter the dining room, King looks at Jamie. "Smells great as usual. Thank you, Miss Jamie!"

Jamie beams, and she and Rusty take their seats at the table. King pulls out a chair for Rita next to his. Following suit, Brett pulls out one of the remaining two chairs and motions for Gabby to sit.

The table setting is simple but graceful. The ivory bone china was custom made for the ranch, hand-painted with the double-horseshoe-crown insignia. A small bouquet of pink tulips in a matching teapot is the centerpiece over the navy blue starched linen tablecloth.

Grace is always said before dinner at the ranch, so King requests that all hold hands and bow their heads. Brett offers his hand to Gabby, allowing her to reach for his. When she does, he interlocks his fingers with hers, smiles, and squeezes hard. She is caught off guard and looks around the table, hoping no one has noticed. She feels silly that this small gesture of affection causes her so much embarrassment. She can feel the heat reddening her face. Briefly looking around the table, she sees Rita's nod of approval, and Gabby knows her shades of red are getting deeper.

Then, she sees Brett and Rita sharing smiles. Gabby shakes her head. *Doesn't anyone close their eyes for prayer anymore?* To her horror, a nervous giggle escapes her throat. It is loud enough to cause her daddy to pause, open his eyes, and look up as if to scold a disorderly child. With a fatherly look and without saying a word, King then bows his head once more and finishes his prayer. All others at the table look up, grinning at each other.

The rest of the dinner progresses without another incident. Much laughter and wine flow, filling the room with gaiety. Their conversation grazes many random topics: the barbecue, horses, oil, cattle, and tennis, then to some of the latest TV programs and novels. Gabby notices that Brett seems at ease with Rusty and her dad, and he appears genuinely interested and knowledgeable about the workings of the ranch. Once or twice, he even refers to his younger years growing up.

After dinner, Brett apologizes for his quick departure, thanking King for the invitation. King shakes his hand firmly and speaks of the cattle branding that will be taking place in a few weeks. "We can use a good rider," King praises, patting him on the shoulder.

Very politely, Brett responds, "Thank you, sir. Call me with the details when the time gets closer."

Wishing to spend a few moments alone with Brett before he leaves, Gabby follows him out to the porch.

"Thanks for coming. I enjoyed our time together," she says.

"Me too," he says, reaching for her hand and pulling her close. Continuing, he speaks quietly, looking into her eyes, "Let's date, Gabby, you and me. We had a great day together, right?"

She looks at him and rolls her eyes. "Me, date you along with at least a dozen other girls. I don't think so." She tilts her head back to see his expression and says, "You go around flirting with everyone, dating everyone. What happens? You get bored and move on." He shifts his weight and avoids looking into her eyes.

Gotcha, Gabby thinks. She then goes forward with her remarks. "Didn't you just have a date with Ella? How did that go for you?"

He smiles. "You're jealous. Admit it, you're jealous," he says again in a singsong voice. He turns her shoulders, so she is facing him. "You know I did that just to make you jealous. Nothing happened. Ask her if you don't believe me. We went to dinner down by the lake."

"How can I believe you? Be honest with me, Brett. Ella tells me there was more to it than dinner."

"Okay, okay, I kissed her. It didn't go any further."

This time she avoids looking at him and continues. She needs to say it and get it out in the open. "We both know what you did to me. How many others are there? Can you at least try to be honest with me? How can I trust someone like you?"

"Come on, Gabby. Here we are, at the circus again. How many times do I need to go over this? It has never happened with anyone else. Sure, I have played the field. Isn't that what a single guy does? It takes two, Gabby. The other women at the club don't seem to have any complaints. I admit, with you, it was different. I am different around you. I wanted you, and I just reacted and—"

"You forced yourself on me," she finishes his sentence for him. She looks up to make sure no one else has overheard. "Whisper—I don't want my dad to find out, okay? It would not turn out well for you, believe me."

Heeding her advice, he speaks in a soft voice, "Come on, Gabby. I apologized. I promised not to let it happen again. I have changed. You have made me want to change. I need you to believe in me. Didn't I back off at the dance? Didn't we have a good time today? God, you are the most confusing woman ever. You send me mixed signals. I'm far from perfect and have my flaws but you, Miss Gabby, are a tease."

She pulls on his arm, yanking him off the porch. They stand in the drive. She opens her mouth to protest, but he starts explaining more.

"I have been trying now for months. I walk you to your car. I buy you flowers. I buy you earrings." He takes his hand and pushes back her hair so he can see them. "I have stayed my distance. I have respected your wishes. Christ, I avoid even looking at you during our drills on the court. Do you have any idea how hard that is for me?" He takes her hand in his. "I can't stop thinking about you. I'm done with other women. I want you. Give me a chance. Surely you can feel the chemistry between us. And about Ella, I know that best friends tell each other everything. I'm not stupid, Gabby."

She allows him to hold her hands. *God, I am pathetic. I have encouraged him. How can he excite me and scare me at the same time?*

"I'll call you," he promises as he first kisses her ear and then finds her lips and kisses them in a manner that is neither quick nor long, just the perfect kiss that echoes *I really like you.* Gabby holds on to his hand as he turns away. It is Brett who lets go of her hand first. With a wave, he jumps into his car, and she watches it slowly drive out of sight.

She stands there a bit longer and gazes up at the night sky. She loves stargazing away from the lights of the city. Tonight is a clear night, and the stars are plentiful. She sends a prayer up to heaven asking God for direction, aware that her feelings for Brett are getting stronger. For these feelings, many will think her crazy. Did other women in Brett's past feel the way she is feeling now? Is all this just part of his charm? How can she ever trust him after their rocky beginning? How can she stand here thinking she is special? He tells her that she is special, but can she believe him? She feels as though what they have shared is real. She is grateful at this moment to be able to spend another day here in God's country. Maybe she will find some answers.

She is so absorbed in her thoughts that she never hears her daddy's steps. She is startled when he places his arms around her and looks up, joining her in stargazing.

"What is going through that pretty little mind?" he chimes. "I know you miss her. I miss her too. Life goes on, Gabby. We need to move on. Your mother would want that for us.

"Tell me about your day with Brett. And what was going on during grace?" King chides, trying to break the intensity.

"Grace ... oh, just something silly, Daddy. I'm sorry. Yes, about

Brett, why did you invite him here this weekend? When did you meet him?" she asks, searching King's face for hints.

"I met him at your art reception. Remember? And when I saw him at the ball in his tux with his cowboy boots, I bought him a drink at the bar, and our conversation led me to invite him to the barbecue," he explains. Gabby is thankful his version coincides with Brett's story, and she is relieved that Brett was truthful. King adds, "You didn't seem to mind. I came out to see him off but did not want to interrupt you two lovebirds," he teases, holding her closer. "Is it over between you and Richard?"

"Pretty much, I just want to be happy. I want to be in love and have a family. Like I was telling you before dinner, you taught me the importance of family, holding that to be more precious above all else. I guess Richard and I haven't been happy for quite some time," she adds thoughtfully.

"He'll try to win you back," King says. "A man doesn't ask a father for his daughter's hand in marriage and just go away. He'll be back. I can't say I blame him."

He gives his daughter another tight hug.

At that moment, Rita comes to the door and calls to them. "Is everything all right?"

King answers, "Yes, everything is great. We were just having a little father-daughter chat. Sorry to be away for so long. Come on, Gabby. Let's have some coffee. Jamie just brewed a pot of decaf."

They turn around, and King wraps his free arm around Rita, escorting both ladies through the front door. "I am one lucky man," he remarks, then proceeds to kiss them both on the cheek.

PART III
The Match

CHAPTER 19

After a cup of coffee, King, Jamie, and Rusty excuse themselves, leaving Rita alone with Gabby.

"Gabby, you and Brett make such a cute couple," Rita says. "What happened out there today? It's obvious to all of us that something is going on to make you blush like a schoolgirl. Tell me! I can hardly stand it."

Gabby, looking down at her coffee, is reluctant to divulge her history with Brett.

"Your father and I put our heads together to figure out a way to get you together. We are so happy it is working out so well." Rita beams.

"You're both in on this! Does Brett know? You have been playing me all along," Gabby remarks sternly.

Hearing her reaction, Rita starts to backpedal, "Oh dear, I've said too much. I thought you were happy."

"Rita, you need to tell me everything, and I mean everything."

Quickly, Rita replies, "Maybe you should ask your father."

"I'm asking you now. What is going on?" Gabby pleads.

Rita reaches across the table and holds Gabby's hand, searching her eyes. "I would never want to say anything that might cause a problem between you and your father."

"Rita, you're my boss, my friend, and now practically family. I really need to know. Please, please," Gabby begs, "tell me."

"Well, over the past year, you shared your concerns about Richard. I saw the heartbreak you suffered. Since you came to the gallery, Richard never has shown an interest in your art. You deserve better. You're a sweet girl. Then, when Brett came into the store, I could see that he liked you and you liked him. It is fun to watch the two of you dance around each other so politely. He's so nice. He came into the store several times looking for you. We would sit and talk, and I could tell by the way he spoke your name that he had feelings for you, so I mentioned something to your father. Wayne checked him out. You know, did a background check to make sure he is on the up and up.

"Your father likes that Brett was raised over on Lohman's ranch. He considers Lohman a good friend and respects his opinion. Lohman had only good things to say about Brett's family: hard workers and good values. Poor Brett, losing his parents at such an early age—first his mother and then his dad. You know, Brett is a fine rider. He won trophies at the local rodeos. I'm surprised you don't remember. You both were about the same age and your family went to all of the rodeos and fairs. You have similar upbringing, similar hobbies—you both play tennis! Your father is in need of someone to look after the ranch. Brett is perfect. He is perfect for you, honey. We're just helping."

Gabby looks down, avoiding Rita's stare. Rita continues to hold her hand and asks, "What's wrong, honey? You had fun today, right?"

"Brett and I have a history and ... well ..." Gabby stutters. "I really don't wish to go into it all." She glances up and sees the hurt on Rita's face.

"If we're going to be family, we should be able to tell each other everything, right?" Rita says firmly.

"It's so complicated and confusing," Gabby confesses.

Rita says in a matter-of-fact, motherly tone, "Talking about it with someone you trust may be just the thing. You can trust me, Gabby. The two of you seem so happy together. Brett's so handsome, so strong, and such a gentleman—"

"Stop it, just stop it," Gabby pleads, tears flooding her eyes. "I know, I know, I know all of that," she blubbers. "That's why it is so hard, and it is so confusing." Taking a deep breath, she blurts out, "He raped me, okay? That's the problem."

Rita shakes her head from side to side. "Today?"

"No. Not today. Months ago. Back in the fall," Gabby answers.

"Oh my, this is a problem. Did you report it?" Rita questions in a calm voice.

Gabby wipes her tears with her hand. "No, no, I was so ashamed. I didn't want anyone to know. It happened so fast. Rita, I didn't say no. I didn't say no," she repeats, hanging her head to avoid Rita's intense stare. "It was like I was paralyzed. Sure, I flirted with Brett. All the girls do. Maybe I did lead him on, you know, encouraged him. It is so confusing." She weeps.

Rita withdraws her hand and sits with both hands covering her mouth and her eyes closed.

Taking a deep breath, Rita says, "Well, this really is a problem." Then she adds, "If your father ever finds out, he will kill him."

"You can't tell Daddy. Please promise me you won't tell Daddy," Gabby pleads.

Rita gets up from her chair and wraps Gabby in her arms.

"I really do like him, Rita. That's why it is so confusing. He has apologized more times than I can remember. He has been so nice. He wants a relationship. I want one too, but how can I trust him? How can I forget?"

Rita does not have an answer. "Gabby, I won't tell your father, at least not tonight. I need to think. This is a tough one. I trusted that boy. When I think of all the conversations we shared... I really liked him. I was beginning to think of him as a son. There must be something we're missing. What you're telling me doesn't seem to fit."

"I know, I know," Gabby whines. "That's why it's such a mess."

Rita gets up from the table and goes to make another pot of coffee. "Before I can make heads or tails out of this mess, you need to start at the beginning. Tell me every detail."

Gabby tells her all she knows about Brett, starting with his numerous affairs with the women at the club and ending with the details that led up to that day behind the curtain on the indoor tennis court.

Gabby glances at the clock. "Oh my, it's well past midnight." She sighs and lets out a deep breath. "I do feel better now that I finally got to tell someone. I have been keeping this inside for months." She gives Rita a hug. "Thanks for listening."

Rita looks at her in a motherly fashion. "That's what family is for. I need to sleep on this one. We'll talk again after I have a chance to sift through everything."

CHAPTER 20

The following morning Gabby sets her alarm so as not to miss breakfast. Guiding her are the smell of coffee and the strong voice of her father.

"Good morning, Daddy ... Rita," she says in a cheerful voice, giving her dad a hug and kissing his cheek from behind.

"Good morning, kitten. You are a ray of sunshine; just look at you," King replies.

Glancing over her glasses while putting the newspaper aside, Rita says, "Morning, Gabby. How did you sleep?"

With glee, Gabby answers, "Surprisingly well. It's so quiet here. I'm glad I was able to spend a few days. I wish I could stay longer."

"Me too," says Rita, "but I have to open the gallery."

Remembering she loaned her car to Ella, Gabby asks Rita, "You mind giving me a ride?"

"Sure, I'm leaving right after breakfast. Remember, the gallery opens at noon."

Gabby smiles and nods. She had wished to stay at least a few more hours; however, she understands the discipline it takes to be a successful small business owner.

After finishing her coffee, Rita excuses herself from the table, giving King some time alone with his daughter. "Coffee on the porch?" he asks, pushing his chair away from the table.

"You read my mind," Gabby answers, filling both their mugs.

When they're seated comfortably on the rocking chairs, King asks, "Tell me, what all do you know about Brett?"

Gabby plays along, knowing her dad probably knows far more about Brett from his investigation than she does. She replies, "Brett ... let's see, he's the newest pro at the club. All the girls have crushes on him. He has a reputation for being a playboy. This weekend, I learned that he grew up over on the Lohman ranch. What do you know about him?"

King takes a sip of his coffee and seems to choose his words carefully. "He seems nice enough. He rides really well. Can't figure for the life of me why he gave it up. Is he a good tennis pro?"

In a matter-of-fact tone, Gabby answers, "Yeah, he's good."

King quickly adds, "Do you like him?"

Gabby remarks, being coy, "Yeah, I like him ... as a pro."

King smiles. "That's not what I was asking. Do you like him?"

Gabby takes a deep breath and sighs. This time, she is the one who picks her words carefully. "It's complicated. Brett has this reputation around the club. When he's with me, he seems sincere. I want to trust him..." Her voice trails off in deep thought.

King notices. "Sounds like there's a 'but' at the end of that sentence. But what?" he asks again, sitting up straighter in his rocking chair.

"I don't know. I just broke up with Richard. I need some time. I'm not ready for another relationship."

King rocks back on his chair. "I can tell he thinks you're fine by the way he looks at you. Tell me about your day yesterday: the picnic, showing Brett the ranch."

Gabby responds, "It was fun. Brett's driving reminds me of you. My insides are still sore."

"Funny you say that," King says. "I see a lot of myself in him. In my day, I was one of the best riders and ropers in the state. And I had an eye for the ladies," he says, grinning from ear to ear. "I played around ... until I met your mother. Well, that was the end of that. I only had eyes for her, never strayed, not one day. Don't be too hard on Brett. He's just finding his way. He comes from a really good family—hardworking, honest Texans. I think the two of you make a great couple."

With his last remark, Gabby almost chokes on her coffee. "Well, there's my dad, once again playing the matchmaker. If I remember correctly, you introduced me to Richard. Back then you thought Richard and I were the perfect couple."

King quickly defends himself. "Okay, okay, I admit it. You and Richard failed to see things eye to eye. Gabby, Richard's making the right contacts, and he's moving up in the ranks. He will make a fine senator, and if he plays his cards right, he will be governor someday. As we spoke yesterday, there are many contractual marriages—marriages for both political and financial reasons. With the help of my money and contacts, I thought you might enjoy being the First Lady of the great state of Texas! You're smart, pretty, and well-educated. Think of all the good you can do, and the people will love you."

He continues rather solemnly, "But you, kitten, you want the fairytale, the romance. Beware. Romance wears thin over the years. Are you sure you're making the right decision?"

Avoiding the question, she asks, "What were you thinking, inviting Brett here this weekend when you knew Richard would be here?"

King grins and faces her before responding. "Being helpful. A little competition always seems to get things moving. It's like a heifer with two bulls. Yes, I picked Richard, but I could see there were problems. Then Rita tells me about this guy named Brett, who keeps coming to the gallery looking for you. She says something about chemistry between the two of you. So, I think that maybe Richard will get his act together, or maybe this Brett guy will prove to be the better of the two. I put them in the same place at the same time. I was always nearby keeping watch. However, my dear, the rules changed a bit when Richard proposed the night before and you turned him down. Basically, the game was the same, just a shift in the rules."

He sits back in his chair after his speech and winks at Gabby. "Brett's a mighty fine-looking man, and he knows his way around a ranch. Like I said earlier, he reminds me so much of myself in my youth. It's a joy watching him ride, effortless. I'm not happy about the tennis thing. No future in that unless you're going to be the next world champion. I can't understand why a man gives up the reins for a racquet.

"Rusty can use some help around here. I'm getting older. I worked hard to make this ranch what it is. I want my legacy to continue after I'm gone."

Gabby looks surprised at her dad. "What about me? I know enough to run the ranch."

King responds softly after seeing the disappointment in his daughter's eyes. "Gabby, you never showed an interest. Sure, you like to come here and play. That's not an interest in running the ranch."

She protests, "I'll hire men to do the work. I can do it, Daddy."

"You have your art. You left for New York City. I'm not blaming you," he replies. "I'm just stating the facts. I support your career. And I understand your need to get away after your mother died. I need someone who understands ranching. I need someone who loves the ranch. I need someone who has the talent and ability to keep this place going. Brett has proven this weekend that he is capable, and if he likes my daughter, and she likes him, well, it's the perfect piece for the puzzle. How do you say it in tennis? Yes, game, set, match."

He sits back on his rocker and gives Gabby a smile, lifting his mug high in the air, obviously pleased.

She sits speechless. There seems nothing more to say. The pair continues to rock on the porch, back and forth, enjoying each other's company. They enjoy the sounds of the day—a hawk circling overhead, the song of a mockingbird, and the occasional whinny of a horse.

Rita's approach breaks the silence, calling, "Wayne, Gabby, I'm sorry to say this, but I need to hit the road if I'm going to make the noon opening of the gallery."

Gabby bids her father farewell and gives him one last hug, whispering in his ear, "We will finish this discussion another time."

"We'll talk later," Rita assures him with a brush of her lips on his.

✦◦❈◦✦◦❈◦✦

Brett arrives at the art gallery exactly at noon, the time Rita requested. There is uneasiness in her voice, which bothers him. His weekend at the King's ranch went great. He can only wonder what causes her urgency. *Maybe it's the painting.* Rita has begged him on more than one occasion to tell Gabby he purchased her favorite Trinity Knot painting; however, the timing never seems to be right. He will reassure Rita that he will follow through on his promise. He is on his afternoon break from the tennis club and is glad he does not have another lesson until later that afternoon. Maybe he'll get to see Gabby when she comes to work later today.

As Brett opens the door, Rita hears the bells clang, and she calls for him to come to the back of the store. She sits on the couch with a cup of hot tea and offers the same to him, motioning him to sit next to her.

"Let me see you," she demands, facing him and taking his hands in her own. "I need to see that dear, handsome face." Then she adds in her well-rehearsed voice, "What did you do to that dear, sweet girl? She says you raped her." Rita squeezes his hands hard with tears welling up in her eyes. Bravely, she continues, "I need to hear your side. I need to hear it from you. Don't lie to me."

Brett, ashamed and embarrassed, shifts his eyes downward, and

Rita knows it is true. She cannot control her emotions. She shakes her head from side to side, sobbing. Still holding hands, Brett squeezes back.

"Rita," he says, "look at me. It isn't like that. It's not what you think. You must believe me. It was a misunderstanding. I never meant to hurt her." He sits earnestly searching for a gesture of understanding, but Rita avoids his stare.

"She never said no. She didn't fight back. How was I supposed to know? I've told her I am sorry a million times. If I could take it back, I would. I would in a heartbeat. I'm shocked she told you. I thought Gabby and I were past this. We had a great time this weekend. What else did she say?"

Rita asks, "But … why? How did this happen? I need to understand. I've seen the two of you together. I know you care for each other." With this, she strokes his face. "Talk to me," she pleads. "Talk to me. I want to know you. Treat you like a son."

Reluctantly and for the first time, he shares his story. He speaks of the horrific experience with his own rape. He tells of his need to leave the ranch, starting over in a new direction.

He talks about tennis and his need to control situations. He holds nothing back, even telling Rita about his frequent sexual encounters, including the raging animal within, and finally getting to the story of sex with Gabby on the tennis court. Rita does not interrupt. When he cannot think of another word to say, he hangs his head and he cries.

Rita grabs his shoulders and hugs him hard. She cradles his head in her bosom and rocks him. That second in her embrace, Brett remembers his mother. He remembers her hugs. He has long forgotten but now, safe and warm in Rita's arms, he remembers and cries harder. First, he cries for the betrayal and fear that his own sexual assault has caused, and then he cries for the deep void that exists from the loss of his family—first his mother and then a few years later his father. He has fought for many years to forget, forcing the hurt deep into the back of his mind, but now, the hurt comes flooding back. He is that lost little boy again and it hurts.

Rita draws him in closer, wraps him in her arms, and cradles him even more. She prays that God will use her to ease Brett's pain. "I'm so sorry," she says softly. "Thank you for confiding in me. Gabby cares for you and wants to trust you. Surely you feel that when you are with her; however, this thing is coming between you. She's afraid of you. You need to show her that you can be trusted. You need to share all of this with her. Don't be ashamed. Tell her. Give her time. She will understand."

Earlier that morning, Rita had dropped Gabby off at Ella's apartment so Gabby could retrieve her car. The girls spent the better part of the afternoon together before Gabby drove home.

As soon as he sees her, Richard starts talking. "I've been waiting for you. We really need to talk. I'm so sorry, Gabby. I know I acted like an ass. I don't want to lose you. We have such a bright future together. Don't take that away from us ... from me."

Hearing these words, Gabby drops her suitcase and repeats his last phrase back to him, "*Take that away from you.* Look at what you have taken away from me. You slept with my best friend. There is no us. You need to move out. Get out of my condo and out of my life."

Richard looks hurt. "Gabby, you don't mean that. I love you. Sleeping with Ella meant nothing to me. I was hurting. I wasn't thinking. I said I'm sorry."

She throws her arms up in the air. "You only think of yourself. Ella thought it meant something. You hurt her, Richard. You don't seem to understand how your actions are self-centered."

He looks at the box he is holding and opens it before continuing, "I saw you on the patio with your tennis coach. It makes me sick thinking about how you kissed him. I was angry and, yes, I slept with Ella. We both have made mistakes so let's stop the stone throwing." He pleads again, "I'm asking for a second chance." He turns the box toward her so she can see the ring. He gazes down at it. "It's a canary diamond, almost eight karats. Don't you want to put it on? See how it fits?"

She cannot believe that Richard is trying to entice her with the ring. She's not that kind of girl. "No, I'm not going to try it on. You already had a second chance, and a third and a fourth. There are no more chances. I don't love you. Just leave, please."

With those last words, she picks up her bags and heads for the door.

"Where are you going?" he demands.

Without turning around, she replies, "Text me when you're gone, okay?" and lets the door slam behind her.

Noticing someone has walked into the gallery, Gabby looks up from her easel and quips, "Good morning, Rita."

"You're here early," Rita says.

"I've been here all night, working," Gabby says after a brief pause. "Richard was still at my condo yesterday so I came here to paint. The time got away from me. Is it noon already?"

"No, no, dear. It is only a quarter past ten. I came early to get some paperwork done," Rita answers after checking her cell phone.

Rita walks around to view the canvas on the easel, and she gasps in astonishment at the abstract painting. "You painted this, just now? It's so dramatic. Even though it is basically a horizontal composition, the slight diagonal gives it movement and energy. And the contrasting colors ... are amazing. I love it!"

Gabby beams at Rita's excitement for the abstract and says, laughing, "Why, thank you. I'm so glad it was worth missing a night's sleep. Painting is such a release for me. I had so much rage and disappointment within me that I needed to brush those feelings away. It felt good to paint and from your excitement, I can tell the energy can be seen in the work."

"It's a good one. I'll sell that one before the end of the day," Rita cheerfully remarks. "I have just the buyer."

Each evening that week after the weekend at the ranch, Brett has stared at the Trinity Knot painting on his mantel. His thoughts drifted immediately to its creator, and he wondered what motivated Gabby to paint it. *What is the mystery behind the trinity knot?* Someday soon, he will ask her.

It is now Friday. Each morning this week when he's picked up his schedule of drills and lessons, he scanned the list looking for Gabby's name. Today, just like the past four days, Gabby's name is absent. The thought of phoning her or texting her is a constant invader, disrupting his thoughts. It is becoming annoying and the few times he does punch her number into his cell, he hangs up before connecting.

Today, even though Gabby's name is absent, Ella's name is there. "God, Ella," Brett says aloud, looking around and hoping that no one else hears him. He really doesn't understand the friendship between the two girls. Maybe their differences are the attraction since they are opposites. Ella is loud, reckless, and flirty while Gabby is classy, reserved, and soft-spoken. If he is seriously considering having a relationship with Gabby, it will serve him well to have a friendship with Ella.

After his informal therapy session with Rita, Brett has chosen to keep to himself. He feels shy and awkward, much in opposition to his usual confident demeanor. Some of his clients have commented on his lack of enthusiasm and zeal. Remarks such as these during a drill spur Brett to feed the balls a bit faster and slightly harder, giving his students an extraneous workout. His unwritten motto is "Make them too tired to complain."

During his lessons, he checks his cell phone at every opportunity, wishing Gabby would make the first contact. Their time together is more positive when she is at the helm. Remembering Rita's advice, he thinks maybe this is a representation of the trust Gabby found lacking in their relationship. He tries to recall every detail of their time together on the ranch, thinking the only awkward moment was when he was playful, holding her down on the blanket. She had leaped away like a frightened fawn. Had he mislabeled this incident as immaturity? But he knows that word doesn't fit the description of Gabby. If he were to ask a dozen people to describe her, immaturity would never make the list. Then there was the conversation on the porch. Doesn't she know that he loves her?

Reality hits Brett hard at that moment, and it hits harder than the round yellow missiles he continues to serve to his clients. Rita is right. Gabby doesn't trust him. She is afraid of him. With all of his own issues weighing him down, he's never thought to place himself in her shoes. He was so busy justifying his own actions that he never really listened to what she was telling him. He heard her, but he didn't listen.

Surprised, he feels a burden lift and he smiles. He realizes his mission. He needs to win back Gabby's trust. He now understands why she keeps bringing up their past. Absorbed with his thoughts and with the adrenaline rush that accompanies them, he feeds a tennis ball a little too hard.

"Ouch," cries Ella. "What are you so mad about? Don't take your anger out on me."

"Anger," he says. "I have no anger, my friend, just a love for the game." He feeds another ball equally hard, and Ella sticks out her bottom lip and pouts when she misses her stroke. Picking up the balls at the end of the lesson, Brett takes care to speak kindly to Ella. She flirts with him as she usually does. However, this time when he returns to the bench midcourt, he feels a hand on his butt. Quickly turning around, he sees Ella grinning and makes a mental note: *Beware. Ella is dangerous.*

During those few stressful days waiting for Richard to move out of her condo, Gabby misses Brett. She misses his smile, and she misses his kiss as well. She is bothered that he does not call her. She remembers his last words to her after their kiss, "I'll call you." But four days have gone by and no word from him. She looks at her cell phone and toys with the idea of calling him. But, no, she isn't going to do that. He said he would call. Her trust meter starts dipping below zero. All the questions and insecurities come flooding back, haunting her. Is he playing her as he has played so many women before? He said he had changed, but has he?

She is starting to worry. At the ranch, she thought they shared something worth continuing. However, at the ranch Gabby also said she was going to get an appointment with a therapist, and she hasn't done that either.

On a brighter note, she is relieved Richard now has moved out of her condo, and he finally quit calling her. During the first seventy-two hours after she asked him to leave, he had called repeatedly. It appears as though he has finally given up, since Ella thoughtfully informed her that she saw Richard yesterday at a local steak restaurant with a recently divorced blonde. Gabby reminds Ella that the woman may be a client, but it really doesn't matter. Ella also mentioned that Brett looked happy during her tennis lesson, and he had flirted with her.

Learning that Richard is out with another woman doesn't cause any reaction in Gabby; however, hearing about Brett flirting with Ella causes the green monster of jealousy to rear up. Inwardly, she is steaming, but outwardly, she acts casually as if Ella has informed her that the sky is blue. The extent of her annoyance is shocking. She is waiting for Brett to call her, and she has allowed herself to trust that he will call. Maybe she is just a silly, silly girl after all.

CHAPTER 21

With Gabby's paintings surrounding on the gallery walls, Rita considers her own knotted mess. Brett confided in her. Gabby confided in her, and King trusts her. Right now, they are the three loops in the trinity knot, and she is the inner circle linking them all together. How will this tangled mess unravel?

You are invited:
Dinner Friday 7 p.m.
Art Smart Gallery
BE THERE!

That Friday evening, Gabby is the first to arrive. Rita offers her a warm greeting. "You look nice," Rita says, giving her a hug. Gabby has worn a simple peach silk dress that accentuates her shapely figure.

"Same to you," Gabby returns the compliment.

"I have a date," Rita chimes, circling so Gabby can see the low-cut back of her dress.

"I wonder who the lucky man is," Gabby says teasingly, then questions, "Is Daddy having dinner with us?"

"Not exactly," Rita offers. "Gabby, I have invited Brett. He has something very special to tell you."

"Rita, I don't think Brett wants an evening with me. He promised to call. I've waited all week," Gabby says, looking sad.

Rita takes both of her hands and demands, "Look at me, child. Trust me. He loves you. He's embarrassed. He doesn't wear it well. I know you see Brett as an overconfident stud, but there's a little boy hidden behind that macho façade. He needs to get something off his chest."

Gabby's mind starts jumping, connecting possibilities, then she blubbers, "Don't tell me Brett slept with Ella. I can't handle more true confessions."

"No, no, nothing like that. Calm down," Rita says. "You're letting your imagination run wild. Here, have some wine." She hands Gabby a glass.

No sooner is the wine poured than Brett walks through the front door carrying a bouquet of flowers.

"How sweet," Gabby says.

Embarrassed, Brett sheepishly addresses Gabby while handing the flowers to Rita. "Actually, they are for Rita. I didn't know you would be here."

Now, Gabby is really confused. Didn't Rita just tell her that Brett has something special he needs to tell her?

Rita places a wine glass in Brett's hand. "Come, come," she instructs, sitting down at the table and motioning the young couple to do the same. After they are seated, Rita offers a toast. "To love," she says, clicking their glasses.

Brett repeats her phrase, "To love." However, Gabby is skeptical and sips the wine, observing the others and wonders what the evening has in store for her.

All three share salad and small talk, but after the main course arrives from the restaurant, Rita looks at Brett and says, "This is your cue to start talking. Tell Gabby what you told me on Monday."

Then she shifts her gaze to Gabby and continues, "Likewise, you need to tell Brett what you told me this week. The lack of communication is the breakdown of most relationships. I know from speaking with both of you that you have feelings for each other. So why don't you just honestly talk? It's really quite simple, and you may even have some fun."

With that bit of advice given, Rita excuses herself, grabs her shawl, and heads out the door. Gabby watches as Rita climbs into King's white Mercedes and drives away.

Now that they are alone, Brett acts shy. "Here we are," he says.

"Yes, here we are," repeats Gabby. "I do believe my dad and Rita are meddling."

"Meddling or not, I do have something to tell you. If I'm going to say it, I need to say it now. Okay? I tried telling you a few months ago when we had coffee, but I wasn't ready." His eyes are pleading and Gabby is thinking the worst again.

He continues, "I have been trying to live with something terrible that happened to me a long time ago. I tried to pretend it didn't happen. I ran from it and I thought with time, I would forget. I never have come to terms with my feelings of hurt and fear. Instead of facing these feelings, I completely changed my life. I left the ranch and picked up a tennis racquet. When your dad asked me to your ranch, my desire to see you and be with you forced me to face those fears. I wasn't going to let something stupid from the past ruin my chances for the future. I completely changed my life once before, and I'm not going to let the events of the past change my life now."

This time, he is able to recall his rape in a matter-of-fact tone. This time he holds his composure; he does not sob or weep. This time, he is able to tell his entire story. He looks into Gabby's eyes. They are full of understanding. He feels no judgment, just sheer, sincere acceptance. His previous feelings of guilt are fading, and for the first time he feels love. Does she know he loves her? Can she possibly love him?

Finally, she speaks, "How awful for you. I know it was difficult for you to tell me, but I'm glad you did. It helps me understand you and even put some things into perspective." She reaches across the table, takes his hand in hers, and squeezes tight.

She takes a deep breath. "Since we are being open and honest with each other, it's my turn." She clears her throat before explaining. "Brett, I keep reliving that day on the tennis court. I never wanted us to have sex. That day I was shocked and overwhelmed. I felt as if

I was paralyzed. I couldn't move and couldn't speak. It has haunted me for months."

She adds, "Similar to what happened to you, I was embarrassed and didn't tell anyone. I didn't plan to tell Rita, but she keeps telling me how nice you are and how handsome you are and, well, I just blurted it out. Sometimes when you and I get close, I get scared. I panic and want to run. Can you understand that?"

"I don't want you to run. I really like you," he responds.

"Against all logical thinking, I have tried hard not to like you," she says. "I have tried to hate you, but that isn't working. You are pretty irresistible, but then you already know that," she teases and continues. "There are so many stories around the club. Some I know are rumors, but you have been with several of my teammates, and I know their stories are true." She pauses and he looks down into his lap. "Yesterday, Ella came to me and bragged that you were flirting with her. What am I to think? You tell me, 'I'll call you.' But you don't. For a relationship, there needs to be trust. I can't trust you. I'm not the girl who has casual sex and then moves on to the next guy. I know I'm crazy to even consider a relationship with you after what we have been through. I am attracted to you, but you scare me."

"I don't want you to be afraid of me," Brett responds. "I know you are the girl any guy would be proud to take home to his family. Since I met you, I don't want other women. And it's Ella who flirts with me. She comes up to me and taps me on the butt. Gabby, I'm just trying to do my job, run a drill, and give lessons. And about that tennis court thing, I don't want that coming between us. Nothing like that will ever happen again."

"I really want to believe you. Really, I do," she says.

"Me too, so ... since we are being completely open and honest with each other, there's one more thing I need to tell you or, better yet, show you. When we finish dinner, can we go over to my place? I promise I won't force myself on you. You can leave whenever you want, okay?" he asks, flashing his big green eyes.

She tilts her head to the side and repeats, "You want to show me something— something that's at your place?"

He answers, "You'll see. I have an idea. Rita said dessert is in the refrigerator. Let's take this carafe of tea and the dessert over to my place. After you see what I need to show you, you can go home. Boy Scout promise," he adds, making the Boy Scout salute with his right hand.

Gabby laughs. "You're so funny. I bet you weren't even a Boy Scout, so what good is your promise?"

"Promise is still good. What do you say?" Brett chimes.

She thinks this will be another test. *I'll let him prove to me that I can trust him. It's better to find out sooner than later.* "Okay, I'll follow you in my car. Then, I can leave whenever I want."

He beams. "Great! Let's get out of here."

He waits for Gabby to come up the stairs to the front door of his apartment before putting the key in the lock. "If I had known you were coming over, I would have cleaned the place a bit," he says. He touches the small of her back, guiding her into the dark apartment. "Here, let me get the light. Are you ready?"

She cannot imagine what she is getting ready for. "Ready as I'll ever be," she answers.

He flips the light switch. Her focus goes immediately to the colorful painting on the mantel. It is the only thing with color in the midst of the modern black and white décor. Her prized Trinity Knot painting is dominating Brett's apartment. Her hand goes to her mouth as she gasps, "How did you get it?"

He answers very casually, "I bought it the night of your reception. I mentioned it briefly when Richard came back. Remember?"

"I thought you were making up something to cover for me," she says.

"I hope you're not upset. I wanted to tell you so many times, but the timing never was right. I wanted things to be right between us when I told you," he confesses.

Not answering, Gabby stares at her painting as if it were the first time, so he continues. "I think that is the perfect place, and I like the way it livens up the entire room. If you think it will be better in another place..." His voice trails away, then he adds, "It's really beautiful. I hope you don't mind that I have it."

Gabby is still staring at the painting, and Brett interrupts her thoughts, "Well?" he asks again.

"Well, what? I'm sorry. I wasn't listening. What did you say?" she replies.

He repeats, "I asked if you were okay with me owning the painting."

Gabby peels her eyes away from the painting. Looking at him, she answers, "Yes, yes, it's fine."

"Now that I have the artist of this amazing work standing right here, tell me about this trinity knot obsession ... the paintings, the necklace," Brett says, retrieving two mugs and two forks from the kitchen so they can sit at the coffee table and enjoy dessert.

Motioning her to sit on the couch, he hands her a plate with the chocolate cake, and he takes a seat next to her.

"Yes, the trinity knot. Tell me about it," he inquires again.

"Well..." she reluctantly responds.

"Hey, I bared my soul to you back at the gallery. Payback," he says, brushing a strand of her hair away so he can see her face. He touches her necklace as if remembering when he held it in his own hands and placed it around her neck so many months ago.

His touch sends a wave of electricity through her. She closes her eyes and takes a deep breath. The nervous habit she developed after her mother died returns as Gabby reaches for the necklace and starts to slide the knot back and forth on its chain. Slowly, she reveals the mystery.

"It was my sixteenth birthday when my mother gave me this necklace." She holds the knot in her hand. "The three loops represent my family, and the circle represents the love that unites us. Then a few years later, my mother was diagnosed with breast cancer and when she died, I really struggled." Gabby has to pause and regain her composure before continuing. "We were really close. I spent weeks mourning. The loss was unbearable."

She stops and chokes back her tears before continuing. "That's when I painted the Trinity Knot series. This particular painting, the one here on your wall, is the painting that with each brush stroke, I felt my mother's presence. It was as if my mother's hand was guiding mine. It was a surreal experience—one that I will never forget."

Absorbed in the telling and careful not to forget a detail, she explains the significance of the colors, especially that the green hue represented healing. She is unaware of the exact moment Brett has reached for her hand and has placed his arm around her shoulders.

When she finishes, he continues to study the painting and remarks, "Now the mystery of the trinity knot is untangled."

"I'm really sorry about your mother," he whispers gently into her ear. He pulls her closer, and she responds by snuggling tighter, feeling his muscles through the fine fabric of his shirt. She tilts her head upward, meeting his eyes, daring him to share a kiss. Reaching over, he strokes her cheek and once again whispers, "You are so beautiful." He accepts her challenge and his lips descend on hers. At first, his kiss is soft and sweet and teasing, piquing her desire, encouraging him for more. Their tongues playfully dance and with each passing second, their need for each other escalates.

As Brett reaches for the remote to soften the lights, he lifts her legs up on the couch as he had done once before. He removes her shoes and starts to stroke her legs. Then he kicks off his own shoes before joining her. They share a soft, playful, teasing kiss that begs for more. She can feel his arousal and this time, she will not deny. She unbuttons his shirt and uses her hands to spread it open, revealing his muscular chest. He reciprocates by cupping her breast, finding her taut nipple through the silk dress. As he slides his hands up her thighs, finding her, she lets out a throaty groan. She reaches for him and feels his hardness as he rests against her thigh. She is breathing heavily and his kiss begins to soften.

"Are you sure?" he asks.

She opens her eyes and mouths the word, "Yes," nodding her head. He needs no further confirmation.

After making love on the couch, Brett carries her to his bed and he slides under the sheets next to her. They lie together entwined. She feels his breath on her shoulder; it is warm and fresh. Resting her head on his chest, she listens to the beating of his heart. Its rhythm is regular and strong, and she prays that her rhythm matches his. Long ago, she read that if two people were truly in love, their hearts would beat in unison. After many months of trying to resist, she has given in to her feelings. She needs to forgive, and she needs to trust. Love is waiting for her, but she needs to embrace it.

She fits perfectly next to Brett. Ironically, she feels safe and warm.

CHAPTER 22

If Brett could sing out to the universe, he would. He cannot believe that he is dating King's daughter and going to the King ranch. He has the top down on his Audi as he drives to Gabby's condo. They are headed out to the ranch to help with spring chores. The cattle need to be moved to another pasture, and the young calves need to be branded, vaccinated, and castrated. He is looking forward to showcasing his skills. He wants to impress Gabby and her father.

Modern-day ranching is a bit different from a few decades ago. All-terrain vehicles have replaced the horse for herding cattle, but a horseman is still needed to separate the calves from their mothers. Being reminded of his love for riding makes Brett realize that in making his decision to escape the bad things that happened to him at the ranch, he was also leaving the past things that he loved as well.

"It feels really good to ride again," he says. He looks at the blond beauty sitting next to him and reaches over to squeeze her hand as they drive along. He smiles at her. "Thank you for getting me back to the ranch," he says, as he knows she is the reason he is able to reclaim his past.

Gabby nods and returns his smile. In all of his years, he never thought he was worthy of getting the chance to date her and be a part of the King world. This is going to be a great day.

It is early morning. They enjoy the quiet before their busy day. That March Saturday, the air is crisp and the patchy sunlight shines on the fields. By the time they arrive at the ranch, King and his men are ready to start work. Brett learned how to cut cattle as a young lad and he prays his skills will quickly return. If not done properly, the calf can get injured. He is also thankful that he was able to get familiar with Frog so that they understand each other, making the job a bit easier. Today his skills will be put to the test.

"Be careful," Gabby says to Brett as she tilts her head back to see him mount Frog. Brett kisses her goodbye and takes his place on horseback among the ranch hands.

"I'll take care of him, kitten," her dad chirps. "You can count on it." He nods. "See you in a bit. I got the men to saddle your horse. When you finish with Jamie, ride on out, and you can help move the cattle."

After hearing her daddy brag about Brett's riding and roping skills, she wants to see Brett in action. But first, she needs to unpack and spend some time with Jamie discussing the plans for her father's wedding. The wedding is only a few weeks away, and there is much work to be done since the ceremony will be held at the ranch.

After taking their suitcases to her room, she finds Jamie in the kitchen.

Jamie's face lights up when she sees Gabby. "Well, hello there, Miss Gabby. You look great ... and so happy!" Gabby's face gets red, and she looks down. "Yes, the look of young love. I haven't seen that look on your face in a while. I am eager to spend some time with that handsome guy with the dimple. Let me see, what's his name?" Jamie teases. Gabby doesn't utter a word, so Jamie smiles as she asks, "Should I be preparing for a double wedding?"

Gabby can hold her silence no longer. "Don't you think that's rushing things a bit? Let's let Daddy and Rita have their special day, okay? Brett and I are just getting to know each other." She looks around the kitchen, "Hey, where is Rita?"

"She's not coming until tonight," Jamie replies. "Besides, Rita trusts us, so let's get down to business. I want this wedding to be perfect."

"Me too!" Gabby agrees.

Jamie gives her the rundown on the plans for the wedding. Rita is doing the invitations and decorations but has left the food choices up to Jamie and Gabby. After deciding on the menu for the appetizers and dinner, it is well past noon.

Jamie looks up from her notebook and says, "I'm sure the men will soon be done with the branding and ready to move the herd. You better get *moo-ving*, girl, if you are helping them."

Gabby puts her hands on her hips and quips, "Aren't you the clever one? See, I'm already dressed." She slaps her blue jeans and lifts her leg to show off her new boots. "I'll see you in a few." She beams back at Jamie as she heads out the door.

◇◆◇◆◇◆◇◆◇

Finally, with the menus planned, Gabby can have some fun riding horses, moving cattle, and seeing Brett in action. She is eager to see him ride and work with her father; however, she will do her best to steer clear from the work being done with the calves. Branding, giving shots, and castrating aren't pleasant tasks, but she knows they are necessary. Separating the calves from their mothers causes stress for both animals, and the bellowing noise they make is deafening. She hasn't helped with herding cattle for many years and sharing this experience with Brett makes it even more special.

Dressed in her riding best, she rounds the barn to find her horse. She hears her father's voice coming from the corral. From his tone, she knows he is angry. It takes a lot to get King upset but when he is, it is best to stay out of his way. However, she still hastens her steps. When turning the corner, she is in disbelief at the scene unfolding before her. King is mounted on his horse and shouting at Brett. *What's going on?* Her daddy uses his rope to lasso Brett around his legs, pulling them out from under him. To her horror, he is dragging Brett in the dirt.

Her father yells, "You're not the only one with skills. I've been doing this long before you were born. How dare you disrespect my daughter?" As soon as these words leave his mouth, King nudges his knees into his horse's sides, encouraging the stallion to quicken his pace. Brett's body turns and twists on the ground.

King does not hear Gabby approaching until she lets out a scream.

"Daddy, stop, you'll hurt him. Stop it," she begs, so distressed she falls to her knees.

King turns to her and bellows, "He'll pay for what he did to you."

Once again, she pleads, "Please stop. I love him, Daddy."

King looks down at his daughter. He shakes his head, looking away from her to Brett.

"You're lucky she wants you alive," King says. "If it were up to me, I wouldn't be so forgiving." He looks once again at Gabby, shaking his head as if asking, *are you sure?* Finding his answer, he reaches for his knife, and he cuts the rope. Glancing back to Gabby once again, King nudges his horse and gallops away.

Gabby wastes no time getting off her knees and climbs the corral fence to get to Brett. He lies motionless in the dirt. "Are you hurt?" she asks, cradling his upper torso in her arms.

"No, I'm all right. Can't say I blame him. Rita told him. He is just defending your honor," Brett says in a matter-of-fact tone Noticing the tears still falling from her cheeks, he reaffirms, "Hey, I'm fine," while wiping her face. Smiling, he flashes his dimple and teasingly adds, "So ... you love me. Guess hearing that makes getting dragged worthwhile. In the future, if we still have a future, remind me never to get on your dad's bad side."

Then he looks into her eyes and says, "Miss Gabby King, I love you!" He pulls her to him and kisses her.

Still holding him in her arms and with tears still streaming down her cheeks, she laughs. "I know it sounds crazy, but I love you too."

Gabby smiles as she descends the curved staircase finding Brett, Rita, and her dad sharing drinks before dinner. She joins them, linking her arms around the two men, relieved that the trauma of the afternoon is behind them.

Rita looks up at Gabby while wringing her hands. "I just could not keep your secret. I felt so guilty keeping something like this from my future husband. Having secrets is no way to start a marriage. I hope you can understand." Rita laces her arm through King's and leans into his body while reaching out to touch Brett's arm at the same time.

Gabby replies, "I hope that we all can move past this. What a day."

King holds his wine glass in the air, addressing Brett. "Yes. What a day. I believe Brett and I have a greater respect for each other after today's events. Don't we, Brett?"

"Yes, sir, Mr. King," Brett answers, putting his arm around Gabby.

She's not sure how the men came to an understanding, but if her instincts are right, Rita had a hand in it. Gabby shifts her eyes toward Rita. Rita winks.

"How's your ankle?" Gabby asks Brett as she glances down. The ankle is wrapped in an Ace bandage and, from the size, she knows the swelling has increased since the last time she examined it.

"I had ice on it until now. It will be fine in a week. It's just a sprain," he answers shyly.

King adds, "We had a great day. All the calves are branded, and the herd is moved to new pasture. I'm tired. It was hard work, but hard work can cover a multitude of sins." He pauses, looking at Brett once again. "Or does the good book say, 'Love covers a multitude of sins'? Well, either way, I think both are right."

Gabby notices Brett standing a little closer to her. She sighs in relief as this day could have easily taken a different turn.

The conversation continues through dinner with everyone sharing his or her favorite part of the roundup. She doesn't blame her dad for confronting Brett. She knows her father's big, over-sized Texas heart was hurting for her and his pride was on the line almost as much as her honor. He had to do something, and he did by taking care of it in his own way. *Maybe the outrageous start to my relationship with Brett will have a happy ending after all.* Is she crazy?

CHAPTER 23

The long-anticipated April weekend has finally arrived—
Saturday is for the wedding preparation, and Sunday will be
the big day. Gabby and Brett arrive at the ranch together early
Saturday morning. In addition to their wedding attire, Gabby's SUV
is packed with fresh flowers, champagne, and the painting she created
for the couple.

The wedding will be small with just immediate family and a
handful of friends. Both Rita's sons will be arriving later this afternoon.
Gabby is eager to meet them as she has heard much about them from
Rita over the past two years. When Gabby was younger, she had always
wished for a little brother or sister, and now with this union, she will
be gaining not just one, but two brothers.

Rita says, "I'm so excited." Her face is flushed, and her eyes beam brightly. This is the first time in the years she's owned the art gallery that she has placed a closed sign on the door for the entire week.

Gabby remarks, "I don't remember a time when I have seen you so happy." Gabby takes pride that she is the one responsible for introducing the couple. "I look forward to meeting your sons. I have heard so much about them, and it will be great to see them and spend some time with my new brothers!"

She's happy that they finish most of the wedding chores early in the afternoon: blue ribbons are draped over the gate and porch railings; flowers are carefully arranged in vases and placed in strategic places, and, lastly, the silver is polished. The caterer will deal with the china and food the following morning.

Gabby is standing on the porch in her appointed spot. Standing opposite her are Rita's sons, who arrived just an hour ago. They are both good-looking: Stan, the older, has broad shoulders while Will is tall and lanky. Stan favors Rita more, but Will definitely has Rita's eyes. Will looks at Gabby and winks and smiles. Brett was introduced to the brothers as her boyfriend, so is Gabby naively thinking Will is just being friendly, or is he flirting with her? She remains quiet and smiles back as they are in the middle of the wedding rehearsal. How these two guys escape having serious relationships of their own makes her giggle as she wonders, *Will it be Stan or Will that Ella will chase after tomorrow?*

Everything comes together as planned. With all the preparations finished for the day, everyone is gathered on the front porch, getting acquainted and waiting for Jamie to announce that dinner is being served. King takes this opportunity to address them. "I want to thank all of you for coming out this weekend to help Rita and I get hitched." He draws Rita tighter next to him. She looks up at him, smiling.

"I want to welcome her two sons, Stan and Will." He lifts his glass in their direction and continues, "Please consider this ranch your home. You can visit anytime. No invitation is required. After tomorrow, you're family." They all lift their glasses to toast, and a small chatter of voices can be heard.

Gabby motions for Brett to get the wedding present they brought earlier. She announces to her dad and Rita, "I was going to give you this tomorrow after the ceremony, but after hearing that speech, it seems that tonight is the perfect time. Open it," she says to Rita and her dad, handing them the beautifully wrapped gift. Rita pulls on the bow and rips the paper, exposing the painting. On the canvas is a knot but not the familiar trinity knot that has graced Gabby's previous paintings. This one is new—it is a zeppelin bend.

Gabby takes this opportunity to explain the painting. "A zeppelin bend is a reliable bend using two separate ropes with four interlocking loops. The two ropes represent our two families. The knot shows the families united, and the interlocking loops represent each of us. I named it 'New Beginnings' since we are all starting a new chapter in our lives."

"It's beautiful, Gabby. Thank you so much," Rita remarks as King walks over to his daughter and gives her a hug and kiss.

"It's perfect," King adds.

"I propose a toast," Brett chimes. "To new beginnings."

In unison, all lift their glasses and toast, "To new beginnings."

Brett looks in the mirror at Gabby's reflection. *She is so beautiful.* He also smiles at the crown on her dresser, reminding him of the snapshot he found buried in the box. He cannot resist and picks up the crown from her vanity, examining each rhinestone. He places it on Gabby's head. She stops applying her lipstick and looks at him in the mirror. He steps back to get a full view, trying to conjure up the image on the photo in his mind to compare. He takes out his phone and says to her, "Let's take a selfie."

Gabby, self-conscious and embarrassed, says, "No, why would we do that? It's silly. My days as a beauty queen are long over."

He looks at her and says, "Nonsense, you are still a beauty queen in my eyes. Let's take the photo, and then I'll explain. Trust me."

She is confused but smiles anyway as Brett takes the picture with his phone.

"What are you going to do with that?" she asks.

He replies, "I wanted an update. Mine is a bit worn."

He takes out his wallet and unfolds the photo that he has carried since he found it at the bottom of the trophy box.

"I thought you might like to see this," he says, holding the photo out to her. She pulls it closer to get a clearer view, then gasps, "How did you get this?"

"It's mine. Been mine for a long time now," he adds.

Gabby stares at him, waiting for more of an explanation. Finding none, she glances back to the photo and says, "Yes, that's me. I was ten. It was the year I was crowned Rodeo Princess."

Brett adds, "Look again. You are only seeing half of it." He smiles at her confused face even after his obvious hint.

She peers at the photo once more, studying the young boy. His eyes are hidden by the Stetson, but she is drawn to the familiar smile. "Is that you? Oh my God!" Studying it more, she continues, "It really is you!"

He gleams, flashing his dashing smile and dimple. "The one and only,"

Then she looks up at him. "Your hat is as big as you." She giggles, pointing to it.

He shifts his weight to see her face as he explains the history of the snapshot.

"Let me see the one you just took," she demands. Standing close together, they look down at the image on the cell phone. Before her is a beautiful couple. The man is dashing in his suit, his dimple a familiar landmark. The woman seated is in a turquoise tea-length dress. Her long hair cannot hide the sparkle in her eyes. Gabby is surprised. Is she really that happy?

"You ready? We had better get downstairs. The wedding will start soon. I need to check on some last-minute details," she says with some urgency in her voice.

"You need to let me check on you," Brett remarks. She stands facing him. He puts his hand under her chin and lifts her eyes to meet his as he has done before. "Beautiful," he says, then adds, "I love you, Miss

Gabby King." Before she has a chance to speak, he pulls her close and lightly kisses her lips. "We have a wedding to attend," he says as he leads her out the door and down the curved staircase.

About the Author

DonnaLee Overly graduated from St Petersburg College, Florida in 1983 with an A.S. in Nursing and she worked as a critical care nurse for 20 years before pursuing a degree in studio art from University of Texas, Austin in 2005. In an effort to mix her art with words, DonnaLee found that clients responded positively to these expressions of emotions prompting her to continue writing with undeniable passion. This encouraged her to finish her first novel that depicts a female character who expresses her emotions through painting.

Her contemporary fiction novels, **The KNOT Series**, are a trilogy written to give a voice to women's issues that are often hushed.

When she's not painting or playing tennis, she's busy writing. Her second novel in the Knot Series, *The Zeppelin Bend* is scheduled to be released in Fall 2018.

Visit the author at her website www.DonnaLeeOverly.com

ACKNOWLEDGEMENTS

This book could not have been possible without the help of many people to whom I am forever grateful.

Thank you to my girlfriends who accepted the challenge as beta readers

Thank you to the experts who shared their knowledge of life on a ranch and rodeo events. You were so patient answering all of my questions.

Thank you to my wonderful editors: Erin Liles for teaching me Creative Writing 101 and to Emily Carmain for making *The Trinity Knot* a better book.

Thank you to my publishers, Marie and Mark, at Giro Di Mondo for helping to make this dream a reality.

A special note of thanks to my family: to my husband for reading the drafts and for his continuous love and support and to my son for saving my manuscripts, just in case.

Look for DonnaLee Overly's second book in the Knot Series

Coming Fall 2018

THE ZEPPELIN BEND

unraveling the knot of deception

Turn the page for a sneak preview

CHAPTER 1

"God, please let this be a mistake." As soon as the words escape her lips, Gabby's body starts trembling. Her fingers lose their grip on the white plastic strip, and it flutters to the bathroom floor. The plus sign is clearly visible against the beige-colored tile. Turning toward the mirror, the pale face that stares back looks foreign and she can't control the whimper that escapes her throat. She sounds like a wounded animal. *Did I make that noise?*

With shaky legs, she lowers herself onto the white throne. She fights tears and chokes back her sobs. She inhales a deep breath and slowly lets it out. These past few weeks, life had been almost perfect. This unexpected turn of events was not in her plan.

Gabby pinches her lips tight and probes the deep corners of her brain. Tracing back the events of the past few months since she has been dating Brett, her tennis pro with his signature dimple, her life and her calendar have been gloriously full. First Richard, her former boyfriend of two years, moved out of her condo. Then she and Brett went to the ranch to help her dad with the cattle branding, and then, they helped with the preparations for her father's wedding. *Think Gabby, think, when was your last period?*

"Pull yourself together," she scolds herself out loud as she stands to flush and cleanup with shaky hands. Then, she smooths her hair and straightens her skirt. She can't hide in this bathroom forever. In just two short minutes, she has learned that her life must take a new direction. Turning the knob, she exits the tiny room. Shutting the door gently she recognizes she's leaving her dreams behind, and entering her new world.

CPSIA information can be obtained
at www.ICGtesting.com
Printed in the USA
FFOW03n1825260318
46065611-46991FF

9 780999 051436